"I can't help it if you're handsome enough to stop traffic," Sierra said with a teasing smile.

"You're enjoying this, aren't you?" York demanded, looking at her with narrowed eyes. "You like making me uncomfortable."

He was suddenly down on the floor beside her, tumbling her backward on the carpet. He was quickly astride her, pinning her arms above her head. His sapphire eyes were full of laughter—and something else she'd never seen before.

She could feel the warmth of his body pressed against her, a heated tingling radiating from wherever his muscular legs touched her slender ones.

The laughter was suddenly gone, replaced by a fierce look of hungry desire that darkened his eyes and filled them with intensity. "Sierra, tilt back your head," he commanded.

She obeyed eagerly, instinctively. "I love your neck," he murmured. "So soft, like velvet . . ." His lips drifted from the tender underside of her jaw to the hollow of her shoulder, leaving little kisses everywhere that fed the fire in her blood, made her gasp. . . .

Bantam Books by Iris Johansen
Ask your bookseller for the titles you have missed.

WHAT ARE *LOVESWEPT* ROMANCES?

They are stories of true romance and touching emotion. We believe those two very important ingredients are constants in our highly sensual and very believable stories in the *LOVESWEPT* line. Our goal is to give you, the reader, stories of consistently high quality that may sometimes make you laugh, sometimes make you cry, but are always fresh and creative and contain many delightful surprises within their pages.

Most romance fans read an enormous number of books. Those they truly love, they keep. Others may be traded with friends and soon forgotten. We hope that each *LOVESWEPT* romance will be a treasure—a "keeper." We will always try to publish

*LOVE STORIES YOU'LL NEVER FORGET
BY AUTHORS YOU'LL ALWAYS REMEMBER*

The Editors

For my good friend Fayrene,
who asked, "Why don't we?"
And for my good friend Kay,
who laughed and said, "Why not?"

Preface

It was said that the Delaneys were descended from Irish kings and were still kissing cousins to half of Europe's royalty. Being more than an ocean away, Europe's royalty could scarcely confirm this.

Luckily for the Delaneys.

Old Shamus Delaney was wont to speak reminiscently of various cattle reivers, cutthroats, and smugglers in his family, but only when good Irish whiskey could pry such truths out of him. Sober, he held to it tooth and nail that the Delaneys were an aristocratic family—and woe to any man who dared dispute him.

They were a handsome family: tall and strong of body, quick and keen of mind. Nearly all of them had dark hair, but their eyes varied from Kelly-green to sky-blue, and it seemed at least one person of every generation boasted black eyes that could flash with Delaney temper or smile with Delaney charm.

None could deny that charm. And none could deny that the Delaneys carved their empire with their own hands and wits. Royalty they may not have been, but if Arizona had been a country, the Delaneys would have been kings.

Whatever his bloodlines, Shamus Delaney sired strong sons, who in turn passed along the traits suitable to building an empire. Land was held in the teeth of opposition, and more was acquired until the empire spread over five states. Various businesses were tried; some abandoned and some maintained. Whenever there was a call to battle, the Delaney men took up arms and went to war.

Many never came home.

In the first generations, an Apache maiden caught a roving Delaney eye, and so the blood of another proud race enriched Delaney stock. Sometime before the turn of this century a Delaney daughter fell in love with a Spanish don who really could claim a royal heritage. She was widowed young, but her daughter married a Delaney cousin, so there was royal blood of a sort to boast of.

They were a canny lot, and clan loyalty was strong enough to weather the occasional dissensions that could tear other great families apart. The tides in their fortune rose and fell, but the Delaney luck never entirely deserted them. They built a true dynasty in their adopted land, and took for their symbol the shamrock.

They were a healthy family, a lucky family, but not invulnerable. War and sickness and accidents took their toll, reducing their number inexorably. Finally there was only a single Delaney son controlling the vast empire his ancestors had built. He, too, answered the call to battle in a world war, and when it was over, he answered another call—this one from the land of his ancestors. He was proud to find the Delaney name still known and respected, and fierce in his newfound love for the land of his family's earliest roots.

But his own roots were deeply set in the soil of Arizona, and at last he came home. He brought with him a bride, a true Irish colleen with merry black eyes and a soft, gentle touch. And he promised her and himself that the Delaney family would grow again.

While his country adjusted to a life without war, and prosperity grew, Patrick Delaney and his wife, Erin, set about building their family. They had three sons: Burke, York, and Rafe.

As the boys grew, so did the empire. Patrick was a canny businessman, expanding what his ancestors had built until the Delaney family employed thousands. Ventures into mining and high finance proved lucrative, and the old homestead, Killara, expanded dramatically.

By the time twenty-one-year-old Burke was in college, the Delaney interests were vast and complex. Burke was preparing to assume some of the burden of the family business, while nineteen-year-old York was graduating from high school, and seventeen-year-old Rafe was spending every spare moment on a horse, any horse, at the old Shamrock Ranch.

Then tragedy struck. On their way to Ireland for a long-overdue vacation, Patrick and Erin Delaney were killed in a plane crash, leaving three sons to mourn them.

Leaving three sons . . . and a dynasty.

One

"Open your coat and get your shirt damp." Chester Brady was gazing critically at Sierra Smith. "We need all the help we can get with York Delaney. He's as tough as they come."

"No way, Chester," Sierra said wearily. "I'm already so wet, I'm practically floating. You open *your* coat and get your shirt wet to play orphan of the storm. Maybe he'll want to take you in from the cold."

She wished she hadn't mentioned the cold. It only reminded her how miserable it was out here in the pouring rain. She wiped the freezing moisture from her forehead, but the gesture was totally futile. More rivulets flowed down her face from her sodden hair. She muttered an imprecation as she remembered that her wet hair was also Chester's fault. He had snatched off the sock cap and thrown it in the cab of his truck before they had left the spot outside of town where the troupe's vehicles and trailers were parked. Chester was nothing if not thorough when setting up his scenes.

"You don't have to be so prickly." Chester actually sounded indignant. "You know I'm doing this to help all of us. Do you think I like going to Delaney, hat in hand, begging permission to come into this godforsaken town?"

"Then why are we here?" Sierra asked. Her feet were sinking into the mud, and she didn't know if it was the mud clinging to her boots or the cold numbness of her feet that was making her stumble. "Hell's Bluff can't have a large population. It's just a little mountain mining town, isn't it?

"A very *rich* mining town," Chester said. "The adjective makes all the difference. We were here two years ago, and it was our best take of the year. Hell's Bluff has one of the richest copper mines in Arizona, as well as being a Delaney property. Those two factors guarantee excellent wages. Then add the fact that Delaney doesn't allow anyone but male mine personnel in the town, and you have the perfect setup for us: several hundred bored, restless miners just aching to spend those excellent wages. The troupe should do a fantastic business."

"Only mine personnel? You mean, no wives or families? How can he get away with such a thing?"

"Money. I told you, he pays better than any operator in the state. He claims women are a disturbing influence in an isolated mountain town like this. So he gives his men one month's leave out of every four to go down the mountain and return to civilization."

"Civilization?" She laughed, and it suddenly turned into a hacking cough. It was a minute before she could stop. Oh, Lord, not again, she thought. The tightening in her chest was frighteningly familiar. No, she *wouldn't* be ill again. It was only because the wind was so sharp here on the side of this damn mountain that it hurt to take a breath. "You make this town sound like it's in the wilds of Africa," she said.

"Not Africa, but it's definitely wild. Dodge City or Tombstone in their heyday would be a more apt comparison." Chester paused, and when he spoke again, it was with grudging concern. "That's a nasty cough you have. You're not coming down with something?"

"No, it's just a cold." She hoped to heaven she was right. She couldn't afford not to be well. As long as she was strong she had value to Brady's Olde Tyme Vaudeville Troupe. She had a place and a purpose.

"You ought to take better care of yourself," he said gruffly.

She almost laughed aloud. Take good care of herself, indeed. Considering he'd done everything possible to see she was thoroughly chilled, the remark struck Sierra as the height of absurdity. Yet she knew he actually meant it. Chester wasn't cruel so much as blindly single-minded about his troupe. He could even be surprisingly sympathetic on rare occasions. "I'll take an antibiotic when I get back to the trailer," she said. "Providing we ever *do* get back. How much farther is it to Hell's Bluff anyway?"

"Around the next turn. Delaney's house is right on the edge of the town."

"Why do we have to ask permission anyway? If you were here two years go, you must have established a relationship with the man."

"It's only courtesy." Chester's glance sidled away. "Besides, Delaney owns the only theater in town."

"I still don't see why you—"

"Well, actually there was a little difficulty the last time I was here," he said uncomfortably. "It wasn't my fault, of course, but there was talk of one of the performers in the troupe operating a crooked dice game in the wardrobe room in the basement of the theater."

"You mean, you were run out of town." It was worse than Sierra had thought. This cold wet trek was going to be totally useless. "Then will you tell me why we're on this blasted mountain in the middle of the night when we could be in Phoenix or Tucson?" The thought of the warm desert country filled her with wistfulness.

"It's not the middle of the night; it's only a few minutes after ten. And the pickings are so good here, it's worth a try. A small traveling company like mine can't compete with the big road shows touring those cities. You know what a rotten take we had in Prescott."

"Yes, I know." She had thought Brady's troupe would go under three weeks ago when a freak ice storm had kept the crowds away for the entire engagement. "But you told me this Delaney was a tough operator. What makes you think he'll have changed his mind about you in the last two years?"

"He probably hasn't, but I'll have to try anyway." There was a hint of grimness in Chester's tone of voice. "Without a good take I can't last another month. I'll be damned if I give up because I've had a run of lousy luck. So you just be a good little girl and sit there in the parlor looking at him with those big black eyes while I try to wring a bit of compassion out of the bastard."

"All right, but that's all I'm going to do. It's up to you to persuade him." It was growing more difficult to breathe. Did she still have any penicillin tablets left in the trailer? she wondered.

"That's all I want you to do," Chester said. "If I'd wanted a woman to seduce the man, I'd have brought Selma. You're hardly equipped for it, Sierra."

She would have smiled, but it wasn't worth the effort. He probably didn't even realize he'd insulted her. Not that she had any illusions about her attractiveness. She had accepted all her assets as well as her limitations a long time before she'd come to work for Brady's vaudeville troupe. "I meant, I won't do any talking."

"No one asked you to talk. But you know damn well your face has an amazing effect on creditors and bribe-hungry sheriffs. It's worth a try with Delaney." They rounded a bend in the road and Chester gestured. "There's Hell's Bluff up ahead. Delaney's place is just past the large pine tree on the left. It's the big Victorian mansion wih all those fancy turrets and cupolas."

The driving rain made it impossible to see anything beyond a few yards in front of her, and she could barely make out the twinkle of lights in the town ahead. Delaney's house was closer, however, and was illuminated by two ornate lanterns on each side of the double doors. The red bulbs in the lanterns glowed garishly over the front porch, turning the white paint a rose hue. "I gather Delaney has a fondness for red," she said. "Those lanterns are really hideous."

"It's probably more an offbeat sense of humor than preference. This building was a bordello during the Gold Rush days of the 1800s. After the gold ran out, Hell's Bluff became a ghost town. When copper was discovered here recently, Delaney restored the original buildings."

"That must have cost him a fortune. He doesn't sound like a very tough businessman." To her intense relief they had reached the porch and were sheltered from the rain if not the cold. A bordello, for heaven's sake, she thought. This was taking on all the aspects of a farce.

"He can afford the whimsy," Chester said dryly.

"He's a Delaney, remember? From what I heard, his brothers were glad to underwrite any expense to get him to take an interest in the corporation when he came home from wandering around the world five years ago." He rang the doorbell. "And the atmosphere here certainly suits him to a T."

"A bordello or a Wild West town?" Sierra asked dully. She didn't know why she was asking questions. She had no real interest in either Delaney or Hell's Bluff. She just wanted this over so she could get back to her trailer and go to bed.

"Both. He's something of a renegade." Chester's brow was furrowed in a frown. "Why the devil aren't they coming to the door?"

"Maybe there's no one at home. We weren't exactly sent an engraved invitation." The irony didn't faze Chester. She doubted he even caught it. *Renegade*, she mused. What a melodramatic word. She supposed it wasn't any more melodramatic than living in a bordello in a ghost town. No, it wasn't a ghost town; it was a boom town now. She had to remember that. She seemed to be having trouble thinking—much less remembering—anything at the moment.

The door was swung open, and Chester stiffened with the eagerness of a spaniel pointing out game. "Mr. Moran. It's good to see you again," he said with bluff heartiness. "You remember me, Chester Brady of the Brady vaudeville troupe? I realize it's late, but I wonder if we could have a word with Mr. Delaney?"

Sierra tried to focus on the small wiry man facing them, but her attention kept wandering away to the lanterns beside the door. They didn't look garish to her anymore but rather warm and inviting. She was shivering. Of course, she was shivering, she thought desperately. It was cold out here. The trembling didn't mean she was going to be ill again.

"I remember you very well, Mr. Brady," said the man who'd answered the door.

Sierra studied him. If he was a renegade, he was a very peculiar one. He was only five feet five or six, with a pale triangular face and light brown hair flecked with gray at the temples. He was dressed in jeans and a bright red shirt that gave his thin frame a bold dapper elegance. It was the eyepatch, she decided. That was why Chester had called him a renegade. He was wearing a black eyepatch over his left eye, and it was definitely a renegade touch. "If you'll wait here," the man said, "I'll see if York will see you."

"Couldn't we come inside?" She hadn't known she was going to speak until the words came out. "It's very cold out here."

The man turned and looked at her appraisingly. His one brown eye was as expressionless as the rest of his face. "I guess that would be all right," he said finally, and for the first time she noticed his British accent. He stepped aside. "As long as you understand I may have to throw you out again, Mr. Brady. York wasn't too pleased with your operation, if I remember correctly."

"All a misunderstanding, Mr. Moran," Chester said. He took Sierra's arm and propelled her into the blessedly warm foyer.

To Sierra's profound relief her shivering stopped instantly. Moran, she thought. She had become confused again. This wasn't the man who was supposed to be the renegade, it was the other one. York Delaney of the Delaney dynasty. Long live the king.

"That's why I'm here," Chester was saying. "I want to straighten out our little difficulty."

"Really?" Moran raised a brow with obvious

skepticism. "I'm sure York will appreciate that. He's such a peaceable man, and misunderstandings completely devastate him." He shut the door. "Wait here." He walked swiftly across the foyer and down the hall.

"Sarcastic shrimp," Chester muttered.

Sierra was getting tired of her boss's tactlessness. Moran was at least three inches taller than her own five feet two. "You can scarcely blame him," she said. "We shrimps have to protect ourselves any way we can from you normal people."

He glanced at her in surprise. "You're a woman. In your case, lack of size is an advantage. It adds to your helpless air."

She clenched her teeth to keep from giving him the answer his sexist attitude deserved. "I never found it gave me any particular advantage."

"Only because you don't exploit it." He grinned. "I knew we'd be able to use you the minute you walked up to me backstage at the theater in Flagstaff and asked for a job."

"Oh, you use me all right," she said, grimacing. She was kept busy from dawn until dark with her regular duties. The hard work was no problem. She enjoyed the feeling of accomplishment it gave her. The only thing she really minded was playing Brady's pitiful waif. Even though *she* knew the role had no relationship to her true self, still playing it grated on her nerves unbearably. Yet if there was a chance this little act could stave off the bankruptcy that constantly shadowed the troupe, then it was worth it. A good many jobs depended on avoiding that shadow, Sierra told herself. Acrobats, snake charmers, and tap dancers weren't exactly in high demand in today's job market. She leaned wearily against the wall. "This time, though, I think you'll come up with a big fat zero."

"We'll see. At any rate it was very clever of you to speak up and get us inside the door."

It hadn't been clever or conniving at all. It had been sheer self-preservation, Sierra mused. But it was no use trying to convince Chester. "It's hot in here, isn't it?" She unbuttoned her heavy corduroy jacket. Funny how wonderfully comfortable it had seemed only a few minutes ago. "I wonder if they've turned up the thermos—" She broke off as a paroxysm of coughing overcame her, leaving her weak and drained.

Chester gazed at her worriedly. "You look like hell. Are you going to be able to work tomorrow? We're going to need every hand we've got to set up in time to open tomorrow night."

"I'll be able to work." She smiled with an effort. "And if I'm a little pale, it will add to the effect you want, won't it?"

"I guess so," he said uneasily. "Have you taken your temperature today?"

She had been afraid to do it, afraid it would tell her something she didn't want to know. She avoided his gaze and tried to evade the subject. "This is quite a place. It reminds me of the Chicken Ranch bordello in that Dolly Parton movie."

Red plush velvet was everywhere. It covered the cushioned bench in the foyer and the circular Victorian loveseat she could glimpse in the parlor to her left. There were even touches of it in the flowered wallpaper. A small crystal chandelier hung from the ceiling right above the curving staircase that led to the second floor. A Titian print on the wall across from her depicted several plump nudes frolicking in a forest glade. Or maybe it wasn't a print, she thought. The Delaneys could certainly afford the real thing.

"I half expect to see a parade of sexy ladies of the evening come trooping down those ornate stairs."

"This is strictly a private residence now," Chester said. "If you want to see a parade like that, you'll have to go down to the Soiled Dove."

"The Soiled Dove?"

"Melanie Dolan's place," he said absently, then frowned. "Look, are you sure you're all right?"

"I'm sure. I'll be fine as soon as I get a good night's sleep." She closed her eyes, thinking she shouldn't be leaning against the wall. Her wet hair was probably dampening the gaudy but no doubt expensive wallpaper. She would straighten away from it in a moment, she promised herself. Soon she would gather enough strength to make the effort. In just another minute she would open her eyes and move away.

York glanced up from his cards as Deuce Moran entered the library. "Trouble?"

"More in the line of annoyance, I'd say." Deuce sauntered across the room to the card table and picked up his bourbon glass. "Chester Brady is waiting in the hall with explanations and apologies." He finished his drink in two swallows and set the glass back down. "And also a request, I imagine."

"The hell he is." York leaned back in his chair. "Why didn't you kick his crooked fanny back out into the storm?"

A distinct look of pain crossed Deuce's face. "I really wish you'd remember we don't all believe in sheer brute force. I prefer to use the persuasion of my razor-sharp intellect and wonderfully facile tongue. Besides, the bloody bloke would make two of me."

York took another look at the cards in his hand, and his lips suddenly quirked. "Judging by these cards you dealt me, it's not only your tongue that's wonderfully facile tonight. Trying to keep your hand in, Deuce?"

A slight twinkle in Deuce's eye belied his deadpan expression. "Why not? You're an advocate of keeping all one's talents and skills honed. You told me so yourself. The stakes weren't all that high."

York chuckled and slowly shook his head. "One of these days I'm going to get annoyed enough with you to remove your other eye. Then what would you do?"

"Use Braille cards," Deuce said calmly. "It might be very convenient. No one would be able to tell if they were marked or not." He paused. "You don't want to see Brady?"

"No. You're the only crook for whom I have any fondness. Use your razor tongue and flick him out of the house. I don't know why you let him in to begin with."

Deuce shrugged. "I don't know either. It was probably the girl. She looked half drowned and there was something—"

"Girl? Brady brought me a peace offering?"

"I don't think so. He would be too sharp to use someone like her to tempt you into bed. She looks young enough to be jailbait, and she's not even terribly attractive."

York's eyes narrowed thoughtfully. "Yet she was intriguing enough to persuade you into letting them come into the house."

"It was the eyes, I think. She has eyes like Liza Minnelli. Big and dark, with eyelashes that look too heavy to lift. They had a most peculiar effect on me."

"It must have been peculiar to sway a hard case like you." York threw his cards on the table. "Why don't you tell Brady to bring in Little Big Eyes so I can take a look at her? It might be amusing, and it's obvious I'm not going to get an honest game out of you tonight."

"I noticed you were a bit restless," Deuce said quietly. "Bored?"

"It's one of the drawbacks of being respectable, I suppose," York said. "Hell, yes, I'm bored." He met Deuce's gaze. "I thought I had it out of my system when I came back to Arizona, but it never really goes away, does it?"

Deuce shook his head. "Too many years of wandering, too many places without laws or even codes of behavior. It spoils a man for the tame life."

"But I was getting bored with wandering, too, before I came back home." He made a face. "I'm tired to death of being the rough, tough mining tycoon. I don't know, maybe I should try something new."

"Maybe," Deuce said. "But Rafe and Burke will be very disappointed if you opt out of the Shamrock Trinity again, you know."

"I know." He'd miss them, too, he thought, if he started wandering. His brothers and Killara were the only part of the Delaney empire he had longed for while he'd been away those seven years. The three of them were linked by ties more binding than heritage and upbringing. Except for Deuce, Rafe and Burke were the only people on the face of the earth York really loved. "I guess I'll have to think about it," he said. "In the meantime, let's see if we can lighten the boredom with your Liza Minnelli look-alike."

"I said the eyes were Liza Minnelli, the rest is an unknown quantity. But that won't be bad in your present frame of mind. You're in the mood for blazing new trails."

"Not with jailbait," York said dryly. "And I doubt very much if the trails in question are virgin-new."

Deuce chuckled as he strode from the room.

York stretched out his legs, his fingers toying idly with the poker chips in front of him. He didn't want to be half a world away from Rafe and Burke again, dammit. Perhaps he was just bored with Hell's Bluff. They had recently opened a new mine in the north of the state. He could transfer its manager here and take over the new location himself. Maybe the challenge would be enough to pierce the ennui he'd been experiencing lately. At this point he'd try any—

Enormous black eyes were burning fitfully in a pale face.

York was so shocked by those eyes, he noticed little else about the girl who had followed Deuce and Brady into the library. Haunting and vaguely melancholy, her eyes dominated the room with the force of a hand laid upon the heart. York felt like shaking his head to clear it of the strangely poignant effect her eyes were having on him.

He found he wanted to *do* something, anything, to chase away her melancholy. Her short black hair was wet and shining, and emphasized the gauntness of her face. Her mouth was her only other noticeable feature, well shaped with a sensitive curve to the lower lip. In the loose dark jacket she was wearing, she looked as tiny and fine-boned as a bird. And she was thin, too damn thin, he thought with an irrational burst of annoyance.

"It's very good of you to see us, Mr. Delaney," Brady said with an ingratiating smile. "But then when I first met you, I knew you were a fair man."

York stood up. "Brady," he acknowledged. His gaze returned to the girl standing by the door. "I don't believe I've met the lady."

"Sierra Smith, one of my employees. She wasn't with us at the time we came to Hell's Bluff two years ago. This is York Delaney, Sierra."

"Mr. Delaney." The girl's voice was low, even a little husky, but expressionless.

For some reason her apparent indifference further irritated York. When he turned back to Brady, there was an added edge to his words. "I can't say my experience with you has been a particularly pleasant one, Brady. You're a greedy man, and I don't care for the breed. My men dropped enough in your coffers without you having to resort to cheating to pick the bones clean."

"That was a mistake," Brady said hurriedly. "The dice game—"

"Was crooked," York finished crisply. He glanced at Deuce. "I have it on the very best authority."

"Well, yes, but I knew nothing about it. The man who was running the game did it without my knowledge or consent. I don't tolerate any kind of chicanery in my troupe. It causes far too much trouble. Now, if you'll just give us your permission to come into town and give a few performances, I promise to keep an eye on everyone and make sure it doesn't happen again."

"I don't give second chances, Brady." York's lips tightened grimly. "My men are isolated here by my own policy. It's my responsibility to see they're not fleeced or victimized because their isolation makes them vulnerable to any huckster who comes along."

"But I assure you, if you'll just—"

"It's no use, Chester," Sierra said. "Can't you see that? Let's go back to the trucks and—" She broke off as a violent fit of coughing struck her.

"Be quiet, Sierra," Brady said tersely. "You said you wouldn't try to persuade him, but don't interfere either."

She was still coughing, and the racking of the girl's fragile body filled York with anger. "Shut up, Brady. What the hell do you mean, dragging her out in weather like this anyway? Can't you see she's sick?" He was across the room in three strides. "Come on, I'll get you something hot to drink before you go back to the rest of your troupe. You're shaking yourself to pieces with that coughing." He took her by the elbow and began to push her toward the door. "Wait here, Brady," he said, glancing back over his shoulder. "I don't want her on her own at this time of night. This is a rough town."

"I'll wait." There was a curiously satisfied expression on Brady's face. "Take your time, Sierra. Mr. Delaney's probably right about your cough. You shouldn't have insisted on coming with me tonight."

The sound Sierra made was somewhere between an incredulous laugh and a gasp. Then the coughing started again, and she was led from the room by York Delaney's far from gentle hand.

Two

"Sit down," York ordered as he opened one of the pine cabinets above the sink. "I'll make this as quick as possible. I don't want you here any more than you want to be here." He took a brand new bottle of lemon juice concentrate from the cabinet and slammed the door shut. After setting some water on to boil, he retrieved a terry-cloth towel from a drawer and tossed it to her. "Dry your hair. You're so wet, I'm surprised you don't leave a puddle where you're standing."

Sierra caught the towel and automatically began to dab at her hair. He was angry, she realized. There was an almost tangible leashed violence to his movements. She collapsed on the kitchen chair he'd indicated and sighed with relief. Her legs were terribly weak, and it felt good to relieve the strain on them.

"You don't have to do this," she said quietly, draping the towel on the back of her chair. "I can get something when I get back to my trailer. I'm used to taking care of myself."

"Then you should have learned to do it better by this time. Why didn't you stay with the others at the trucks?" His back was toward her, and it seemed taut with anger and disapproval as he measured lemon juice into the cup. It was a beautiful back, she thought hazily. He was wearing a black chambray shirt, and it emphasized his broad shoulders and narrow waist. His low-slung jeans were faded to a pale white-blue and clung to muscular thighs and the most magnificent tush she'd ever seen.

But then the attractiveness of his back wasn't really unusual when you considered the rest of him was just as beautiful. When she'd first walked into the library, she had felt an almost physical shock. His classical features could have graced a Grecian coin, Sierra thought, and his startling sapphire-blue eyes were clear and deep against the darkness of his sun-bronzed face. His thick raven-black hair had just the right amount of wave. It wasn't fair for a man to be this gorgeous, she thought; Mother Nature should have spread her bounty around more evenly. The only hint of imperfection was the cynical twist to his perfectly shaped mouth and the slightly jaded expression in those wonderful blue eyes.

"Well?" He turned to face her.

Had he asked her a question? She tried to concentrate, but the fog of lethargy creeping over her made it increasingly difficult. Oh, yes, now she remembered. "Chester wanted me to come with him."

"So you obediently trotted out into the storm with a cough that sounds close to tubercular," he said caustically. He poured hot water into the cup, then walked over to her, the cup and saucer in his hand.

"He thought I could help," she said. "I think he's getting desperate." She took the cup he handed her. "Chester doesn't realize there are some people who can't be influenced."

He went still. "You agreed to try to 'influence' me."

She smiled shakily. "Not that way. Neither Chester nor I are stupid enough to think you'd be sexually interested in me. But Chester believes I have a kind of lost-puppy appeal that can soften up a certain kind of businessman. Sometimes it even works."

"You've let yourself be used like this before?"

"On occasion. The troupe isn't in very sound financial shape, and there are a lot of good people with their jobs on the line." She lifted the cup and the steam rising from it was filled with the pungent scent of lemon.

"Don't just stare at it. Drink it," he said as he dropped into a chair across the table from her. His eyes were blazing in his set face.

What she had said had evidently made him even angrier. Well, it didn't matter. He had already made up his mind anyway. She took a sip of the lemon juice. It was hot and sour and cut through the haze of congestion as it flowed down her throat. "This is very good."

"My mother used to dose my brothers and me with hot lemon juice when we had colds. I don't know if it did any good, but it always made me feel better."

She took another sip and gazed at him over the rim of the cup. Even when frowning, he was handsome enough to stop traffic, Sierra mused. He was like a magnificent peacock whose plumage rippled and swayed in the breeze, revealing new colors and vibrancy every moment.

"Why the hell are you looking at me like that?" he asked testily. "I assure you I'm not one of those businessmen who can be 'softened' by a big-eyed waif."

"I know. I was thinking you remind me of a peacock." Oh, dear, what a thing to say. The words had just tumbled out.

He blinked in surprise. "A peacock?"

"Because you're so beautiful," she said. "It's really not fair, you know. There are so many plain people in the world. You shouldn't have gotten it all."

He was instantly wary. A come-on? he wondered. He knew he was physically attractive. It had been a miserable curse when he was growing up on the ranch. Later he had found it useful and even exploited it when it suited him. He was accustomed to women enjoying looking at him, but he didn't remember anyone ever gazing at him with the grave wonder he saw in Sierra Smith's eyes. No, it wasn't a come-on. Her expression held a childlike honesty and directness.

He pulled his gaze away from hers with an effort. "How old are you anyway?"

"Twenty-one."

"You look younger. Deuce thought you were jailbait." He studied her. "How did you get hooked up with Brady's outfit?"

"Eighteen months ago I was working as a bank clerk in Flagstaff when Brady's vaudeville troupe came to town. When they left town, I went with them."

"If you wanted to become involved in show business, I think you could have chosen a better vehicle than Brady's sleazy outfit." His lips twisted in a crooked smile. "Is life on the wicked stage as glamorous as you thought it would be?"

"I wasn't looking for glamour." She took another sip of the lemon drink. "You know, when I was a kid, my family traveled constantly, and I dreamed of a time when I could have everything orderly and secure. Then, when I finally achieved my orderly life-style, I couldn't stand it. It was too regimented. I wanted to try new things, experiment. I swore every single day I was going to learn at least one new thing."

"And did you find you could do that with Brady's troupe?" His gaze was fixed intently on her face.

"Yes, and I don't think you're being entirely fair to Chester. The troupe may be a little sleazy and this kind of entertainment may have gone out with Stutz Bearcats and raccoon coats, but his people love performing. Chester provides them with an opportunity to do that, an opportunity they wouldn't be able to find anywhere else." She set her empty cup down on the table. "Thank you for the drink, Mr. Delaney. I'm sorry to have bothered you." She started to get to her feet. "I'll go tell Chester I'm ready to go."

"Sit back down." His voice cracked like a whip. "You don't look like you can hold your head up, much less hike in mud and slush. I'll phone one of the men to drive the two of you back to your trucks." He opened the door, then looked back over his shoulder. "Is Brady really running an honest show these days?"

She nodded. "There's never been any trouble as long as I've been with the troupe." She made a face. "Other than with creditors and local magistrates wanting their license money."

"Whom you obligingly 'softened' for your kindly employer."

She met his gaze steadily. "Sometimes."

He cursed beneath his breath and strode from the room.

Ten minutes later Chester was bustling her solicitously out the front door and into the back of a Jeep driven by a brawny miner who introduced himself as Jake Bowdin. The Jeep started with a jerk and spewed mud in all directions as it sped out of town and down the mountain.

"You get right to bed when you get back to your trailer," Chester said. "And sleep late tomorrow. We can do without you until afternoon."

She looked at him in surprise. "You can?"

"We wouldn't want Delaney to think we were misusing you. He told me in no uncertain terms I should take you home and see you were properly cared for." His smile deepened with satisfaction. "Right after he gave me permission for a three-day run in Hell's Bluff. You did a good night's work, Sierra."

"I had nothing to do with it." She was stunned. She had been sure when Delaney had stalked out of the kitchen, the issue was closed. "No one could persuade York Delaney to do anything he didn't want to do. He must have believed you when you told him the episode two years ago was a mistake."

"Perhaps. However, we'd better cover all our bases. I'll get Myra to fix you a hot toddy when we get back tonight, and you stay in bed tomorrow morning and nurse your cold."

"I don't need a hot toddy. I've already had something." Steaming hot lemon juice his mother had made for him when he was a boy. What had he been like when he was little? It was strange to think of that fantastically beautiful man being coerced by anyone to do anything. There was a restlessness, a recklessness, seething just beneath the surface, and she sensed it could be ignited by a breath of a spark.

Still, there had been a rough kindness in his attitude toward her tonight. Or had it been pity? She stiffened in automatic defensiveness, then relaxed. No, not pity, thank heavens. There had been too much anger and leashed tension for him to have entertained an emotion as gentle as pity. She felt an intense surge of relief. Lord knows, she'd had enough of that particular commodity in her life. She rested her head wearily against the Plastine window of the Jeep and closed her eyes. She was too tired now to worry about what Delaney had felt or not felt toward her.

It didn't matter anyway. Splendid peacocks had no place in her life. She would mark this interview down as the new experience of the day and forget about it. But at least this experience had one good outcome. She had a little time now to rest and get rid of this blasted cough.

Deuce came back into the library and shut the door. "Well, they're off. Big eyes is tucked cozily into the Jeep and on her way to a safe warm bed." He lifted a brow. "Though the way you took over and rushed her out of here, I wasn't sure you didn't mean her to occupy yours tonight."

York didn't look up from the game of solitaire he was playing. "Why should you think that? You were right, she was more like a drowned puppy than a femme fatale." He slapped a ten on a jack with the faintest hint of violence. "And she looks about fifteen. I would have felt like a child molester."

"Did you find out how old she is?"

"Twenty-one." He slapped another card down. "A bank clerk who threw up her nice safe job and succumbed to the lure of the footlights. Incredible."

"Do you believe her?"

"Hell, yes, I believe her. It's too bizarre a story to be anything but the truth. *She's* too bizarre to be anything but authentic."

"A fact that appears to irritate you a tad." Deuce sat down across the table from him. "I'm curious to know why."

"Why should it irritate me? I've never had a passion for strays. It was always Rafe who brought home the wounded birds and motherless calves."

An expression of gentleness flickered across Deuce's face. "Oh, I don't know. You brought me home. If I remember correctly, I was something of a wounded animal myself at the time."

York looked up and smiled faintly. "The only wounded animal you resembled was a tiger with a sore paw. Roaring ferociously at the temporary indignity, but always knowing he'd be king of the jungle again once he'd healed."

Deuce shook his head. "You persist in equating my prowess with your own. I may roar, but I don't bounce back quite so readily. I needed help and you gave it." He saw York frown with discomfort, and immediately switched back to his usual mocking lightness. "Not that anyone wouldn't have done the same. Charming ne'er-do-wells such as myself are almost an extinct breed and should be treasured accordingly." He watched York play for a minute. "You're not concentrating. You missed placing the seven of spades on the—"

York growled something definitely obscene, tossed the deck of cards on the table, and pushed back his chair. "That's it. It's not enough you cheat me blind, now you criticize my solitaire game."

"I detest carelessness in any game of chance. Even the most casual contest should be handled with grace and dexterity, every move like the cape work of a great matador."

York fought a smile as he stood. "I can appreciate

the comparison. There are certainly elements of deception in both your game and that of a matador."

"You're going to turn in?"

He nodded. "I'm in no mood to play bull to your matador tonight." He walked to the door. "I may call Josephson at the Pino mine tomorrow morning and get a progress report. The last I heard, they were moving slower than I'd like."

"Everyone moves slower than you like. You were born two steps ahead of the rest of us."

"No, I was born two steps behind everyone else." York grinned. "Now I have to go faster to make up for everything I've missed."

"Well, you certainly do that." Deuce stared speculatively at York. "Why *are* you letting Brady bring his show into town?"

Something flared then faded in York's eyes. "The men will like it. You know how boring it can get up here at Hell's Bluff. If there's any gambling, you can keep your eagle eye on him to make sure it's an honest game."

"Is that the only reason?"

"What other reason could I have?" As Deuce continued to gaze at him without answering, he shrugged with barely concealed exasperation. "How the hell do I know why I did it? It was an impulse. Maybe I was just bored enough to welcome a little trouble in my life."

"Could be." Deuce started gathering up the cards. "Brady will toe the mark. I'll see to it. Good night, York."

"Good night."

Why had he decided to let Brady come into town? The question was like a thorn prodding York as he climbed the stairs to the second floor. He'd had no intention of giving in when he'd walked out of the kitchen tonight. He'd been as surprised as Deuce when he'd told Brady he could start moving his troupe and sets in at dawn tomorrow. It *must* have been an impulse that had provoked such a weird—

Rising Star.

He had turned the corner of the landing and the portrait was suddenly there on the wall before him. He stopped short as shock rippled through him. Why hadn't he connected the two before? Probably because the portrait was such an integral part of his life and he had always taken it for granted. Yet the great dark eyes looking out of the portrait were undoubtedly Sierra Smith's eyes. The Apache woman's body was not quite as slender, her bone structure not as delicate, but the spirit was exactly the same. Strength and resilience mated with a poignant loneliness and terrible isolation.

It was crazy. The painting had been done in another century of a woman from a different world and culture. There was no real similarity. Yet as he tore his gaze from Rising Star's portrait and resumed climbing the steps, he knew he was lying to himself. And he knew why he'd given Brady's troupe permission to come to Hell's Bluff.

Three

"It's about time you got here, Sierra," Chester said
when he walked backstage. He'd just introduced
the first act of the evening, and the Great Marinos
were swinging into action. The spotlight was on
Gino, poised on the seesaw. His brother, Roberto,
was standing on Papa Marino's shoulders. "Where
have you been? I sent Snooks for you more than
thirty minutes ago."

"I was in the wardrobe room mending Zelda's
costume," Sierra said. "I came as soon as I could."
The audience roared with approval as Gino did a
double somersault and landed on his brother's
shoulders. Sierra had never seen a more enthusi-
astic audience than the miners of Hell's Bluff. For
the past two days they had packed the theater each
afternoon and evening and gave every evidence of
enjoying themselves tremendously.

"I need you to groom the dogs for Reva's act,"
Chester said, "and then fill in for Maureen with the

snakes. She's been throwing up all evening. She won't be able to go on." He frowned with disgust. "What lousy timing for her to get sick tonight."

"The snakes," Sierra repeated vaguely. She was so tired, it was difficult to think.

"What the devil is wrong with you? You've performed the snake act before."

"Right." She turned away. "I'll go now."

"No. The dogs first," Chester said, exasperated. "Didn't you hear me? Reva needs the dogs groomed. We're all working ourselves into the ground to put on a decent show so Delaney will let us come back. You *might* give us a little cooperation, Sierra."

Anger flared within her. "I have been cooperating. I've worked from dawn until after midnight for the last two days. I've fed the animals, repaired costumes, sold refreshments, picked up trash, filled in with the acrobat act, collected tickets—"

Chester held up his hand. "Okay, okay. I'm sorry. I guess we're all under a bit of pressure." He smiled. "Now, be a sweetheart and run and groom the dogs. In another four hours it will all be over, and we can relax."

She sighed, her rage dying as quickly as it had come. It was too much effort to maintain anger, when she needed all her strength just to keep going. "I'll groom the dogs."

It took almost an hour to groom and beribbon Reva's three poodles and four spaniels to perfection. Then Sierra hurried down the hall to the dressing rooms.

"Good evening, Miss Smith."

The words were spoken in a familiar precise British accent, and Sierra turned to face Deuce Moran. He was leaning against the wall, dressed as the other men in the audience in uniform of boots, jeans, and bright colored shirt. However, he wore them with a matchless panache. It wasn't the first time she'd seen him since the show had opened three days ago. He had unobtrusively drifted around backstage, his one brown eye dagger-sharp in his expressionless face. He had smiled and bowed with the faintest hint of mockery whenever she had glanced at him, but hadn't spoken to her until now.

"Brady appears to be reaping a bonanza tonight," he said.

"Yes, we're doing very well." She brushed a lock of hair from her eyes. Her forehead was damp with perspiration, and the fine dark wisps persisted in clinging to it. "Chester is very grateful to Mr. Delaney for giving us this opportunity. We all are."

"The troupe may be doing splendidly, but I'm not sure about you." Deuce straightened and strolled toward her, taking a handkerchief from his pocket. "You have a smudge on your cheek." He carefully wiped it away. "And I hate to be so rude, but a distinct doggy odor hangs about you."

"It doesn't surprise me. I've been grooming Reva's dogs. I'm sorry I can't stay and chat, but I have to change. I've got to go work the snakes."

"Now you're grooming snakes?"

"No, I'm filling in for Maureen, the snake charmer."

"You appear to do a good deal of filling in." He gazed at her searchingly. "I believe you're even paler than the night I first saw you. Are you quite well?"

"Quite," she said with a smile. "I'm only a little tired. We've all been pushing ourselves for the past few days." She turned away and waved casually. "Perhaps I'll see you later, Mr. Moran."

He watched her hurry down the hall. Her back was straight and as determined as her smile had been. His lips pursed in a low soundless whistle.

."That was a very gallant gesture," York drawled, looking at the handkerchief in Deuce's hand. "For a moment I couldn't believe it was you, Deuce."

Deuce turned to watch York's approach. "I was having a few problems believing it myself. I'm not accustomed to avuncular emotions coursing through my cynical veins." His smile was self-mocking. "It was a cumulative effect, I assure you, or I wouldn't have acceded to it. She's a very appealing child."

"Cumulative?"

"I've been watching her tear around here for the last three days, wearing herself to a state of exhaustion." His smile faded, then disappeared entirely. "It bothered me."

York frowned. "They've been overworking her? I told Brady to send her to bed."

"If he did, she was out of it again by the time the show opened the first day."

York muttered a curse, his gaze on the dressing room into which Sierra had disappeared.

Deuce shook his head. "Don't be so fierce. If she'd been that much of a victim, I would have been tempted to step in myself. The girl was more than willing. She was running around helping everyone. It appears she's a cross between a universal understudy and a maid of all work." Deuce smiled. "She was even the target for Simon the knife thrower last night. They may be using her, but it's with her full consent and cooperation. I'd say in this case she's her own worst enemy." He lifted a brow. "I'm surprised you haven't shown up sooner than this to check on Brady and his menagerie."

"Why should I do that? I knew you would have everything under control."

"No reason. I just somehow thought you would.

Instead, it seems almost as if you've been avoiding the place."

"You're probing, Deuce. Cut the amateur psychology. I was busy, dammit. I don't have time to go to a vaudeville show."

"No? It's been my experience you make time for anything you want to do." Deuce held up his hand. "All right, I'll drop it. It's only my damnable curiosity. You know I suffer from the affliction of an inquiring mind."

"Yes, I do know." A smile tugged at York's lips. "You have the reputation of being particularly inquisitive regarding other players' hands."

"True. It's been a constant source of trouble for me since early childhood." Deuce stuffed the handkerchief into the back pocket of his jeans. "I think I'll go sit down out front and keep an eye on our little waif. I didn't like the way she looked a bit ago. It wouldn't surprise me if she's running on pure stamina and guts at the moment. Would you care to come along? She's evidently going to indulge in a little snake charming to amuse the audience."

"I might as well. I don't have anything better to do. It might be interesting to watch you act as guardian angel." York kept his tone deliberately offhand as he fell in step with Deuce.

Snakes? he mused. What kind of snakes? If what Deuce said was true about her varied duties, she wouldn't have had time to gain any significant amount of expertise. The act might even be dangerous. He smothered a quick leap of fear as deliberately as he'd smothered the nagging temptation to come to the theater for the past two days. Why should he be worried about Sierra Smith? he asked himself. The girl meant nothing to him. Her resemblance to Rising Star, as well as the courage and honesty she'd revealed, would naturally intrigue him, but not to this extent. Yet if he hadn't known Deuce had been constantly on the spot, he wouldn't have been able to resist coming himself to make sure she was all right. Now it seemed Deuce had been calmly standing by and letting the idiotic girl make a damn martyr of herself. The knowledge ignited an anger that effortlessly pierced the casual facade he was trying to maintain. His voice was suddenly sharp with irritation. "Why the hell didn't you stop her if you were so concerned?"

"Because it's none of my business." Deuce paused before adding softly, "Is it, York?"

"No." The word came out a little jerkily. "She's old enough to take care of herself, even if she isn't bright enough. You're right; it's none of our business."

Fifteen minutes later as he was sitting in his third-row seat watching Sierra begin her performance, York found that the avowal of lack of responsibility did nothing to diminish the turbulent emotions racing through him.

She was thinner. He hadn't thought she could get any thinner. The harsh spotlight made her skin appear parchment-pale, and her lips were pinched and strained even as she smiled at the audience. She was dressed in navy-blue satin harem pants and a filmy white long-sleeved blouse. A wide red sequined sash cinched her tiny waist. She looked like an Arab street urchin as she reached into the straw basket on the stage in front of her.

"I want you to meet a friend of mine," she said, lifting an enormous snake from the basket. "This is Bathsheba, a python who comes to us from Morocco." She paused and moistened her lips. "She is over six and a half feet long and kills her prey by constricting her coils about it and squeezing it to death." She draped the snake about her shoulders and it immediately wound itself around her. "At least she used to do that. Now she's very docile and affectionate, as you can see."

"She doesn't look very docile to me," Deuce whispered. "I've always hated snakes. Slimy bastards."

The python didn't look very docile to York either. The thick muscular coils wrapped about Sierra's slender body made him feel sick. She didn't appear frightened, though, and was handling the snake as if it were a fox fur. Maybe there really wasn't any danger. Lord, he hoped not.

She was still speaking, but her words were oddly halting, as if she had to think before each one. "Most people think snakes are cold . . . but it's . . . not true."

"There's something wrong with her," Deuce murmured, staring intently at Sierra's face. "She's swaying like a drunken sailor up there."

York could see what he meant. Sierra was gazing blindly at the audience, and she seemed unaware of the monstrous snake hugging her. She shook her head as if to clear it.

"They're really quite warm," she went on. "After the show I'll bring Bathsheba to the edge of the stage and let a few . . . of you . . . touch . . ." Her lids fluttered, then closed entirely. Her knees buckled, and she fell to the floor.

"That's not part of the act," York muttered as he leaped to his feet. He started down the aisle toward the stage. "She's fainted, dammit!"

"Hell's bells!" a miner in the first row cried. "The python's constricting!"

York's gaze flew to the small limp form on the stage. The python had apparently been startled by the jarring fall and was acting with instinctive defensiveness. It was tightening its body around Sierra's neck and shoulders, forming a noose.

"Sierra!" With one leap York was on the stage,

his hands tearing at the thick mottled body of the python. "Deuce, help me. I can't get a grip on the damn thing. Grab the other end." He could feel the powerful muscles of the snake flexing beneath his tugging hands. Sierra hadn't stirred since she'd fallen. Were the coils around her throat already asphyxiating her?

Deuce was pulling at the tail, an expression of extreme revulsion on his face. "Snakes. Lord, I hate snakes. Why couldn't it have been the knife thrower causing all this bother?"

They finally managed to pull the python, which was still writhing, off her.

"What do we do with it now?" Deuce said. "It's rather like having a tiger by the tail, isn't it?"

"Throw it back over there on the far side of the stage."

"Gladly."

They released the snake, and it slithered over into a corner.

"Get one of the stagehands to put it back into its basket while I see what damage it's done." York didn't wait to see if his order was carried out, but dropped to his knees beside Sierra. She hadn't regained consciousness, but she didn't seem to be having trouble breathing. Perhaps they had freed her from the python before it had done any more than bruise her. The delicate skin of her neck was already marked.

"Is she all right?" Deuce asked. He was standing beside him, a frown creasing his forehead.

"How the hell do I know?" York asked huskily. "I don't think the snake really hurt her, but I can't be sure. And who knows why she fainted to begin with?" He was gathering her in his arms and standing up as he spoke. "Well, we're damn well going to find out. Contact the company doctor and have him meet us at the house."

"I understand show people like to take care of their own," Deuce said quietly. "Hadn't we better try to find Brady in that crowd in the wings before we cart her off the premises?"

York's arms tightened protectively around Sierra's slight body. "He's had his chance. I'd say he's done a damn lousy job of taking care of her, wouldn't you?"

"Possibly," Deuce conceded with a slight smile. "I assume this means you've changed your mind about the girl not being your business."

"Yes." York turned away. "I've changed my mind. Get the doctor on the double."

There was a haze of deep red floating over her. Where had she seen that exact shade of red before? It had been very recently, and if she could only pull her thoughts into some sort of order, she was sure she would remember. The haze solidified and transformed itself into a velvet canopy. When she was a little girl, she had always dreamed of having a bed with a canopy, she thought vaguely. She had imagined that sleeping beneath a canopy would be like being held in a loving, protective embrace. There had been times in her childhood when she had been lucky to have any sort of bed at all. More often than not, she'd had to share a pallet on the floor with her sisters.

"Are you going to look at that canopy all day?" The deep voice was as familiar as the red plush. Her gaze flew to the man sitting in the spindly red Louis XIV chair by the bed.

Brilliant blue eyes set in the face of a Greek god. York Delaney's face. She felt no surprise. It seemed perfectly natural to wake up and see this incredibly beautiful human being lounging casually beside her. It was all of a piece with velvet canopies and childhood dreams that had never come true.

"No," she said, "I'd rather look at you. You're much prettier."

He made a face. "I wish to heaven you'd quit saying that. I'm not accustomed to people blurting out their appreciation of my physical attributes. It reminds me of the times when I was a kid and tried to find a way to break my nose so the other kids would quit teasing me."

He would have been as stunning as a child as he was as an adult, she thought. It must have been difficult for a boy who had the sun-touched glamour of an Apollo to survive among the cruelty of children. She could sympathize. She'd been one of the different ones too. "I'll try to remember," she said.

"Do that." He leaned forward. "Look, the doctor has pumped you full of sedatives and antibiotics, and he said you'd be a little disoriented when you woke up. I didn't want you to be frightened." He placed his hand over hers. It was warm and protective despite its hardness, she thought dreamily. It was rather like the canopy above her. "Do you remember the snake?" he asked.

She had to concentrate for a moment, but it began to come back to her. "Bathsheba."

"When you collapsed, your reptilian friend decided you were the enemy and tried to squeeze you to death. Deuce and I managed to pull her off before you were more than bruised."

Sierra frowned. "Is she all right?"

"Is *she* all right?" York drew a deep exasperated breath. "I just told you she tried to strangle you, and you're worried about the snake."

"She wouldn't have meant to strangle me. She's really very gentle. You didn't hurt her, did you?"

He was silent for a moment as if counting to ten.

When he spoke, he enunciated every word very carefully. "No, we didn't hurt her. Perhaps you'll be more concerned when you see the bruises on your neck and shoulders."

"You can't blame any creature for obeying its instincts." Her gaze was traveling around the room. "I'm at the Chicken Ranch, aren't I?"

"Chicken ranch?"

"No? I guess that was another bordello." She rubbed her forehead. "I think I am a little confused."

He nodded. "The sedatives. Don't worry about it. You're at my place at Hell's Bluff. The doctor examined you and said you were suffering from severe bronchitis and exhaustion."

"Bronchitis? Oh, that's wonderful!" she said happily.

"Bronchitis is wonderful?"

"I was afraid it was pneumonia again. I was hospitalized with it just before I joined the troupe, and I thought I'd never get over it." Her smile was tremulous, but brilliant. "But it's only bronchitis."

"Which could have slipped into pneumonia with the greatest of ease the way you were pushing yourself."

"But it didn't, and now it won't. Isn't that wonderful?"

He looked at her glowing face and suddenly his expression softened. "Yes, it's wonderful," he said gently. "But the doctor says you have to take better care of yourself from now on. Eat balanced meals, rest more, not drive yourself so hard."

"Oh, I'll be fine in a few days. I'm very strong really." She covered a yawn with her hand. "You'll see. I'll bounce right back. I always do."

"You're getting tired. We'll talk about it again when you wake up." He leaned back in his chair.

"All right, whatever you say." He was right, she thought. She was getting so drowsy, she could hardly keep her eyes open. "You don't have to stay, you know. I'm used to being alone."

His hand tightened on hers. "Are you?" His voice was a little husky. "Well, I'm not. Maybe you won't mind if I stick around for a while?"

Her fingers curled around his hand with the confiding affection of a small child. Her eyes closed. "No, I won't mind. I think I'd like . . ."

Bright morning sunshine was streaming through the red velvet curtains. This time when Sierra opened her eyes, there was no haziness. Her mind was bright and alert, and she was definitely dismayed.

"May I come in?" a voice called. The door opened to reveal Deuce Moran. He was holding a covered tray. "I knocked, but I guess you didn't hear me."

"I just woke up." She scrambled to a sitting position, then looked down apprehensively as the red satin coverlet fell to her waist. She breathed a sigh of relief when she saw she was wearing her own faded gray cotton pajamas. At least she was decent. "Your knock must have awakened me."

"I figured you would need food more than sleep by this time." He walked into the room and set the tray on her lap. "Even with all those vitamin shots the doctor has been giving you, I decided enough was enough. You start in on your orange juice and I'll get you a washcloth to wipe your face. It will make you feel better." He was gone for only a moment, and instead of handing her the washcloth, wiped her face himself as if she were a child. "There."

"Thank you." She grinned. "This is getting to be a habit. I'll have to try to be tidier and save you the bother."

"No bother." He tossed the washcloth on the bedside table and sat down in the chair beside the bed. "I'm getting quite used to it."

He sounded terribly British at that moment, Sierra thought. "Are you from England?"

His lips quirked. "Oh, you've guessed I'm not a native of this wild and woolly West of yours? Now, I wonder how you figured that out. Berlitz assured me my lazy cowboy drawl was almost perfect."

"Just naturally perceptive, I suppose." She took a bite of toast. "Well, are you?"

He nodded. "Liverpool, originally, but I regard myself as a citizen of the world." He made a grandiose gesture with one arm. "Naturally the world is immensely grateful for my condescension."

"Do you work for Mr. Delaney?"

"Everyone in Hell's Bluff works for York in one way or another. I'm acting as his personal secretary at the moment."

"But it's more than that, isn't it? You're friends."

"Yes," he said quietly. "We're friends." He smiled. "You are perceptive, Miss Smith."

"Sierra. I understand you saved me from strangulation. That fact should surely put an end to any formalities between us."

"York saved you. I merely assisted. I detest reptiles." He grimaced. "If I hadn't been afraid York would murder me if I didn't do as he ordered, you might have been uncomfortable for quite a bit longer, or at least until I got up enough nerve to touch the bloody thing."

"I doubt that."

"Don't doubt it. I'm not the stuff of which heroes are made. Some men are meant to fight dragons; other men are meant to tell the tale. York is the dragon fighter." He smiled faintly. "Though I've never seen him fight one over a helpless maiden before."

She looked up swiftly, her fork halting in midair.

"I'm not helpless. I'm a little weak at the moment, but there's no way I'm helpless."

"Tell that to York. It takes a bit to get his protective instincts aroused, but once done, it's like a tidal wave." He smiled wryly. "Take it from one who knows."

"I will tell him." She put her fork down and started to move the tray aside. "Where is he?"

"Steady." Deuce set the tray back on her lap. "Let's not go off half cocked. He's down at the mine. He's been here with you for the last three days and he thought it behooved him to check in."

Her eyes widened. "Three days?"

"The doctor wanted you to rest. He's been keeping you sedated."

She couldn't believe it. "I've been here for three days? What about the troupe?"

"Gone. Two days ago."

She felt swift panic rise within her. "What do you mean, gone? They *left* me?"

"They had no choice. York was a bit . . . irritated with Brady when you collapsed. So irritated that Brady felt compelled to close down immediately after the show and scamper out of town while York was still getting the report on you from the doctor."

"But they couldn't have just left me," she whispered. "They *need* me. Did Chester leave a message?"

"Oh, yes. He sent your clothes and said he would be in touch with you later and give you the troupe's itinerary."

"Later? But what am I going to do now? I don't have a job."

"You're going to rest, just as the doctor ordered," Deuce said gently. "You needn't worry. York will take good care of you."

She ran her fingers distractedly through her hair. "What do you mean? I can't take anything

from him. He's a stranger." She drew a deep
breath. She had to keep calm. "Please tell Mr.
Delaney I appreciate his concern, but I don't accept
charity. If you'll let me know where my clothes are,
I'll get dressed and be on my way."

Deuce shook his head. "The doctor said at least a
month's rest before you take on any work. Probably
a good deal longer before you resume the marathon
you were running with Brady's outfit. Now, eat
your breakfast."

"I'm not hungry."

He sighed. "Look, love, what difference does it
make if you let York support you for a week or so?
Do you know just how rich the Delaney brothers
are?"

How could anyone in Arizona help knowing? she
wondered. The Delaney dynasty had been a legend
for generations, involved in mining, ranching, and
far-flung business enterprises. You couldn't drive
down a street in Tucson without seeing the Shamrock logo stamped on trucks and buildings, or
open a newspaper without finding references to
fabulous Killara—the Delaney homestead—or the
famous Shamrock Horse Ranch.

How long, Sierra asked herself, had she known
about the Shamrock logo and the Delaney dynasty?
The dynasty, she knew, had been founded in the
early eighteen hundreds by a colorful Irish immi-
grant, Shamus Delaney, who had begat generations of equally colorful descendants. And Sierra
was well aware of how rich they were, for the activi-
ties of the Shamrock Trinity, the last three surviv-
ing members of the dynasty—Burke, York, and
Rafe—figured almost as much in the gossip col-
umns as on the financial pages.

"I know how rich they are," she said. Her lips
tightened. "It doesn't make any difference. Charity

is charity. I earn my way. If I don't give, I don't take."

"York isn't going to like this."

"You're damn right, he's not." She looked up to see York standing in the doorway. "And he's not going to put up with this nonsense either." He jerked his thumb. "Leave us alone, will you, Deuce? I'll talk to her."

Deuce stood up. "I hope you have better luck than I've had," he said as he passed York. "She's a very stubborn woman."

The door closed behind him.

"Now, let's get down to cases," York said. He strode across the room. "I gather you're balking at staying here and being sensible."

"I earn my way," she repeated, her face clouding mutinously. "It's very kind of you to—"

"I'm not kind," he interrupted. "Nor particularly gentle. And I'm certainly not gallant. I want to make that quite clear. When I first saw you, I wanted nothing to do with you because you aroused all sorts of incomprehensible emotions in me. I don't have any use for those emotions. I like my life exactly as it is. When I'm involved with a woman it's sex, pure and simple." The look he gave her was as direct as a saber thrust. "If you'd like to pay me in that particular coin, I'd probably accept it."

Her breath stopped in her throat. "Sex?" Her voice was so faint, she was scarcely audible. "You want to have sex with me?"

A smile tugged at the corners of his mouth. "Why are you so surprised? You must have been propositioned before. You're not a child."

She moistened her lips with the tip of her tongue. "I'm not sexy. Why would you want to go to bed with me?"

He sat down on the bed beside her. "I obviously

have very esoteric tastes. I find the idea of making love to you extremely erotic. The first night I saw you, I lay in bed afterward and thought how tiny and fine-boned you were; how tight you'd be and how careful I'd have to be not to hurt you."

She gazed up at him with helpless fascination.

"You have eyes that mirror every emotion," he went on. "Do you know that? I thought about what they'd reflect when I touched you, moved over you." His voice dropped to just above a whisper. "And I thought about how we'd look together when we made love, how white and soft you'd be." He glanced at her hand lying on the coverlet. "How small and delicate your hand would look as it moved on my thigh and over my—"

"Stop." Her hands flew to her flushed cheeks. "You're . . . joking. Aren't you?"

"Am I?" His expression was totally inscrutable. "What makes you think I'm joking?"

"Because you're . . ." She broke off and fluttered her hand. "And I'm . . ."

"Well, you certainly make everything crystal-clear." He raised his brows. "You don't want to pay me in that way? Pity. I thought I had the perfect solution."

She shook her head. "I'm not a prostitute," she said absently as her gaze searched his face. "You were kidding, weren't you? You could have anyone. Why would you want me?"

"I thought I'd been quite eloquent on the subject." He got to his feet. "Never mind. We'll forget about it. I promise not to harass you while you're here recuperating." He strolled toward the door. "Just relax and concentrate on getting well."

"Mr. Delaney."

He stopped with his hand on the knob and looked back. "It's customary to call would-be seducers by their first names. You wouldn't want to give us undue illusions of our respectability."

"But that isn't the case this time, is it?" Her voice was clear and challenging, though her expression was still uncertain. "You just pulled this feint to catch me off-guard and get me to resign myself to living off your charity for the next few weeks."

"Did I?" His gaze was suddenly warmly intent as it moved over her. "I suppose you'll have to decide that for yourself. Did I sound as if I was kidding?"

"No," she whispered. Her eyes were enormous in her thin face.

"Then don't count on it, Sierra. Not for a minute." The door closed behind him.

She drew a deep quivering breath and tried to relax. She felt as if she'd been picked up and tossed about by a cyclone. The curious fluttering in her stomach and the tightness in her chest had nothing to do with bronchitis. York's words had jolted her into an awareness of herself that completely stunned her.

She had known she wasn't actually ugly, but hadn't considered the possibility there was anything about her to foster a strong attraction. She had always evoked protective feelings in men. She had been the kid sister, the daughter, the pal. Now, with frightening suddenness, she was being looked upon as a desirable woman.

She hadn't experienced the slightest self-consciousness around York Delaney because she had never considered he would feel different from any other man she had encountered. He had been like a beautiful statue or an exquisite but remote figure on a movie screen, someone with no real connection to her life.

Now she was shaken and electrified and so aware, it was painful. She mustn't feel like this, she told herself. Men of York Delaney's ilk didn't develop sudden passionate obsessions for mouse-like creatures like Sierra Smith. He was merely tossing her something else to think about to divert her from making plans to leave. Deuce had said York was very determined when his protective instincts were aroused.

No, York's proposition had definitely been a trick, she decided. A well-meant trick, but deceit nevertheless. She mustn't think anything else. She had to block out her sexual awareness of him. She would concentrate instead on how to bail herself out of this humiliatingly dependent situation. She picked up her fork and began to eat slowly and with determination. She wasn't hungry, but whatever plan she decided upon would require all her strength.

York paused outside the door, releasing his breath slowly in a little explosion of tension. She hadn't believed him. He didn't know whether he was relieved or indignant. For that matter he didn't know what the hell he would have done if she had taken him up on his proposition. She had been so upset about her precious independence being compromised that he had spoken on impulse. He had succeeded in distracting her with his offer, but the price might be higher than he wanted to pay. Sierra was capable of touching his emotions in any number of bewildering and tempestuous ways, evoking tenderness, possessiveness, even anger.

Dear Lord, the tenderness was incredible. There had been moments in the past few days when he had ached with it. Of course, that wasn't the only ache he'd known since he had met Sierra. How could raw lust and this exquisite gentleness exist side by side?

He didn't want either one, dammit. He had lived

his entire adult life doing exactly what he wanted to do, when he wanted to do it. He had no desire for ties or restrictions of any kind. Hell, he should be thanking his lucky stars that Sierra hadn't believed him. If his erotic fantasy had suddenly become reality, who knows if he would ever have rid himself of this obsession? Now at least he had breathing space to try to regain his sanity.

He started down the stairs. The sensible thing to do, he told himself, was to see as little of Sierra as possible until she was well enough to leave Hell's Bluff. Avoiding her shouldn't be too difficult. He would keep himself busy during the day and spend his evenings at the Soiled Dove, and with any luck . . .

He was so intent on formulating his plans, he didn't notice that all the way down the stairs he never once looked away from the hauntingly poignant portrait of Rising Star.

Four

"What are you doing?" Deuce asked when he entered the bedroom. Sierra was sitting on the edge of the bed. "Get back under the covers. I thought it was too good to be true when York told me our little problem was settled for the moment."

"I was just going to take the tray downstairs." York's "problem" was indeed taken care of, she thought ironically, but not the way he'd figured. "I can't seem to make my legs work right. I'm as weak as an infant." She swung her legs back on the bed and pulled the sheet up. "I'll have to try again later."

"I'm glad something is managing to influence you into behaving sensibly." Deuce stooped to pick up the tray from where she had set it on the floor. "I'll take the tray back to the kitchen." He nodded approvingly. "You've cleaned your plate quite nicely. York will be pleased."

"I didn't do it for York. I did it for me," she said

quietly. "You and York seem to be under the misconception that I'm a scatterbrained child. I ate because I need strength to do what I have to do. I need information to do that as well. Will you come back and talk to me after you've taken the tray downstairs?"

He regarded her thoughtfully, then nodded. "I'll be back. You're proving to be a very interesting houseguest, Sierra."

He was true to his word and sauntered back into the room fifteen minutes later, carrying a tea tray. He set it on the bedside table and proceeded to pour two cups of tea from the earthenware pot. He grinned as he handed her one of the cups. "Have you ever noticed how we return to the simple comforts of childhood when we're under pressure? I haven't felt the need for a nice cup of tea for months."

She smiled. "I don't intend to pressure you. I just want to know my options. If I ask any questions you don't want to answer, just tell me to go soak my head."

"And risk throwing you into pneumonia? York would assassinate me. I'd be safer answering the questions." He waved his hand. "Go ahead and interrogate me."

"I need to know the setup here. I have responsibilities and I don't have any money. I'll have to get a job. Chester said this was a company town, and mining was the only industry. Is that right?"

Deuce nodded. "Delaney Enterprises owns the whole kit and caboodle."

Sierra nibbled on her lower lip. "There has to be some other service-affiliated companies here. What about a restaurant or a diner?"

He shook his head. "York built a dining hall down by the mine. It's open twenty-four hours a day. He hired a first-class cook and staff, and the food is better than most of the restaurants in Tucson." He paused. "And the food is free. He provides it as a company benefit. No private restaurant could compete with such a sweet setup."

"I can see that." She frowned. "Entertainment?"

"There's the theater, which is used only on rare occasions, and a satellite dish brings in all the cable TV shows. There's a giant screen in the dining hall, and York has the latest video cassette movie releases flown in every week."

"The doctor?"

"Is hired by the company and so are his assistants."

"Why do I feel I've wandered into a minor monarchy?" she asked gloomily. "There has to be something." She looked up suddenly. "Chester mentioned some place. . . . What was that name?" Her face brightened. "The Soiled Dove."

Deuce suddenly looked wary. "And just what did he mention about that particular establishment?"

"I don't quite remember. I was pretty much out of it that night. I think I was running a fever." She made a face. "Don't tell me York owns that too?"

"No, he leased the building to Melanie Dolan. He has nothing to do with the running of the Dove."

"Is it a bar? That's a very interesting name."

He inclined his head mockingly. "Thank you. I suggested it myself to Melanie. I thought it fitting."

"Fitting?"

"The name has a certain colorful historical significance."

"Do you think I could get a job there?"

He looked a little startled. "I don't think York would like that. In fact, I'm sure he wouldn't."

"Too bad," she said coolly. "If this is the only show in town that doesn't have the Delaney name on it, then I can't be choosy. There has to be something I can do. I learned to be very adaptable working for Brady's troupe."

"Well, adaptability is certainly a quality Melanie insists on in her help," he said, clearly amused. "Forget it, Sierra. It won't do at all."

"Why not? A hard worker is always in demand. What I lack in experience, I'll make up in enthusiasm."

The amusement turned to outright laughter. "Considering your determination, I think there's every chance you would become the belle of the establishment." He chuckled again. "I'd almost give my eyepatch for York to see you at Melanie's."

"Good. Then will you introduce me to this Melanie and vouch for me? I know you can't give me a reference but—" She broke off with a frown. "Why are you laughing? I'm very serious."

"That's why I'm laughing." He leaned back in his chair, his shoulders still shaking. "You're obviously not a Regency scholar, Sierra. Would you like to know just how the term *soiled dove* was used?"

She sighed. "I think I'm beginning to guess."

He nodded. "A lady of the evening, a cyprian, a light-skirt."

"It should have been obvious," she said wistfully. "I guess I got a little excited. It's not a bar?"

"Oh, but it is. When Melanie leased the building, York insisted it be kept as authentic as the town. So Melanie decorated the lower floor as a saloon that would fit quite nicely back in the Old West. Melanie's 'ladies' are dressed up as dance-hall girls, and they play the part beautifully. A man can go in and have a drink or a game of cards." He paused. "Or anything else he wants."

"I gather the Soiled Dove is far more popular than the nightly movies in the dining hall?"

"I believe that would be an accurate surmise."

"But Chester told me York was opposed to having women in Hell's Bluff. He said York believed it caused trouble."

"Only a certain kind of woman—the kind a man becomes emotionally involved with," Deuce said. "He's right, you know. I've seen it in the mining camps in South America and Africa. Men get tied up in knots over a woman they want and can't have. When a woman makes herself available to everyone, no jealousy exists and therefore no trouble."

"Rather simplistic."

"As I said, it appears to work."

Her brow knitted in a frown. "There might be some work I could do there besides the obvious," she said thoughtfully.

He straightened swiftly, the amusement abruptly gone. "No, Sierra. The Dove may be honest, but it's rough as hell. It's no place for you. York would—"

She gestured impatiently to silence him. "I'll have to think about it. I can't do anything immediately anyway. I'll have to recover a little first."

He began to relax. "Very sensible."

"But I'll have to start paying York back for my medical treatment and my keep right away. I suppose he has all the domestic help he needs about the house?"

"Sierra . . ." He shook his head. "Don't you ever give up? No, as a matter of fact, he doesn't have a housekeeper. There's a contretemps regarding an old family servant who's presently staying with his brother Rafe. He won't have the woman here, but in order not to hurt her feelings he can't replace her either. So instead of hiring someone, he has our meals sent up from the dining hall and Melanie's maid comes in once a week to give the place a good cleaning. The rest of the time we do for ourselves."

"He can't replace a housekeeper because it might hurt her feelings?" Sierra asked blankly. "And this is one of the flint-hard Delaneys I've heard so much about?"

"This is *York* Delaney. He's not a one-dimensional man. You'll find that out, Sierra."

"I may not have time to discover anything about him." A strange wistfulness flickered through her. "I've been far too much trouble already. I've got to get back on my feet and off his hands."

"We'll have to see about that." He stood up. "Now, finish your tea and see if you can take a nap. I'll be back in another few hours to expose myself to another third degree. I'll bring a deck of cards." He didn't look at her as he carefully set his cup on the tray and picked the tray up. "By the way, do you play poker, Sierra?"

"No, I've never learned."

He looked at her swiftly, and his smile shone with sudden sharklike brilliance in his triangular face. "No matter. I'll teach you."

"Just what the hell do you think you're doing?" York's voice was laden with exasperation as he stood in the middle of the kitchen looking up at Sierra.

Her heart gave a little jerk, then started to pound in double time. She drew a deep steadying breath but didn't turn around. "Putting down fresh shelf paper. There's no use in scrubbing down kitchen cabinets and then putting back the old paper. Besides, this check design goes much better with the pine cabinets and looks much more 'Old West' than—"

"Get down from that ladder."

"In a minute. This is the last shelf, and then I'll be—York!" He had grabbed her from behind and was swinging her off the ladder. Then he plunked her down so she was sitting on the cabinet beside the sink.

Their eyes were on the same level, and his were blazing. "Dammit, why were you crawling all over the place on that ladder? Don't you have any sense?"

"It's precisely because I do have sense that I was using the ladder," she said reasonably. "How do you expect me to reach those upper shelves without one? We all can't be giants like you."

"I don't expect you to use a ladder at all. I don't expect you to be scrubbing shelves. I expect you to be lying in bed recuperating, dammit!"

"I did lie in bed," she said crossly. "For an entire week—which was four days longer than I intended. I would have been back on my feet last Wednesday if it hadn't been for that poker game."

"Poker game?"

She nodded. "Deuce taught me how to play poker and insisted no game was complete without proper stakes."

York's anger was immediately arrested. "What kind of stakes?"

"Well, I didn't have any money so he suggested we play for hours."

"Hours?"

"It got kind of complicated. We were betting the hours I'd stay in bed without complaining. Before I knew it, I'd lost a hundred and seventy-two hours." She frowned. "You know, I think he cheats."

"Really?" A faint smile tugged at his lips. "That's a very serious charge."

Sierra's eyes narrowed shrewdly. "He *does* cheat."

York nodded. "Superbly. He was a professional gambler before we came together in a little mining camp outside Barranquilla. Unfortunately he regards deception as one of the integral facets of the game. It's made his career both interesting and extremely hazardous."

"Did you put him up to doing it this time?"

"I knew nothing about it." His smile faded. "Not that I wouldn't have approved of any measure in this case."

"Like the one you used?" She hadn't meant to ask that question, darn it. She had intended to ignore any mention of that last unnerving conversation with him. She had been right to take his words with a grain of salt, she told herself. She had seen nothing of him for the entire week of her stay, which certainly didn't argue for his having a flaming passion for her. Probably the queer aching that knowledge had brought had caused her to blurt out the very question she had meant to avoid.

"But I didn't use any deceit," he said quietly. "I only suggested and you refused."

His eyes were only inches from hers and she felt as if she were drowning in them. Such beautiful eyes, Sierra thought, clear and deep and all-encompassing. Perhaps she *was* drowning. She didn't seem able to breathe, and her head was spinning dizzily. "You didn't mean it," she said.

He became very still. "Would it have made any difference if I had?"

Would it? she asked herself. It was hard to think with his body so close to her own. The top button of his blue shirt was open and she could glimpse the mat of springy hair on his chest. He smelled of soap and a pine-scented after-shave that was deliciously outdoorsy. She found herself leaning closer and breathing more deeply as if to take more of him within her. The vaguely erotic thought jarred her into a semblance of sanity. "No." The word wasn't as firm as she would have liked, and she cleared her throat to rid her voice of its huskiness.

"Besides, I knew all the time that you weren't sincere."

"And how did you know that?"

She wished he'd move away. His body heat seemed to surround her and caused a tingling, throbbing sensation in the pit of her stomach, the palm of her hands, and the sensitive crests of her breasts. She moistened her lips. "Just look at me. I'm a plain brown hen to your peacock. There must be a hundred bird-of-paradise types you could nest with."

"Why do I feel we've been transplanted into a meeting of the Audubon Society?" He frowned. "What ever gave you the idea you were a little brown hen?"

"I have a mirror." She shrugged. "It doesn't matter that I'm not pretty. I have intelligence and stamina, and that's probably more important than being attractive."

"It's nice that you can be philosophical about it," he said dryly. "I wish you were a meek little hen. It would make things a good deal easier for me." His hands were suddenly cradling her face. "Listen, I don't know where you got the idea you're not attractive, but it's not true. Do you know what I see when I look at you? I see character, sensitivity, and vitality." His thumbs rubbed the lines of her cheekbones with a soothing, mesmerizing motion. "And I see eyes I could look into for the next hundred years or so and never get tired. Your skin is velvet-soft and meant to be touched, and your body . . ."

She didn't think she'd have the breath to speak but somehow the words came out. "I knew we'd come to the brown-hen part eventually."

"Because you're not built like Raquel Welch?" He slowly shook his head. "I've never had a fondness for Amazons. You're as soft and delicately made as a robin. I'm half afraid to touch you for fear you'll break." His voice lowered to just above a whisper. "Do you know how tempting it is to touch and handle something that's exquisitely formed and fragile? In museums they're careful to put those pieces under glass. Not only because of their value, but because it's natural to want to touch, to run your hands over every curve and hollow, to feel the texture and the sleekness."

Again she felt she was drowning in his eyes. "We're back to birds again. I'm a robin, not a brown hen?"

"You're a robin," he said gently. "And I meant every word I said to you, even though I shouldn't have said it. Because robins should have safe, secure nesting places, and I'll never be that, Sierra. Not for any woman. I'm too restless to ever settle down. The minute I feel the walls closing in, I run to a place without walls."

Renegade. The thought pierced the haze of intimacy he had woven about her. He was warning her. She was tempted to deny the warning was necessary. Such denial might salve her pride, but she couldn't do it. He was trying to help her, and the warning *was* necessary. She was trembling on the brink of something she knew was entirely outside the bounds of her experience. "I'll remember that."

"And I'll remember to try to keep my hands off you." His fingers moved gently, compulsively, on the soft hollows of her cheeks, then dropped away. "It won't be easy. Now I know why the Greeks become so obsessive about their worry beads. I think I could get the same sensual pleasure from running you through my fingers."

Instinctively she looked at his hands. They were very strong, tanned, and graceful with long sensitive fingers. She could imagine those fingers moving with pleasure over smooth amber beads, caressing the texture, enjoying the solid shape.

They would move just as sensitively over a woman's body, weighing the softness, the tips of his fingers tracing a pattern. . . .

"What are you thinking about?" His eyes had narrowed with heated intensity.

Wild color flooded her cheeks. "Worry beads."

He muttered a curse. "The hell you were." His hand impulsively reached out toward her, then stopped in midair before he touched her. "You've got to help too, dammit. We could go to bed together and have a fantastic time and progress toward an equally fantastic affair." His expression was hard and unflinching. "And that's exactly what I want to do. But I couldn't promise you it would last forever and I don't know if you could survive a breakup, Sierra. You're not cut out for short, meaningful relationships that are really elongated one-night stands." He took a deep breath. "And I'm not cut out to watch you suffer because I can't be what you want me to be. So help me, okay?"

"Okay," she whispered. She was silent a moment, then forced a smile. "Well, will you help me down off this cabinet? I promise I'm not trying to seduce you."

His hands grasped her waist and he lifted her to the floor. His palms were warm through her cotton T-shirt and she felt an odd tingling spreading through every vein. The pulse was jumping erratically in the hollow of his throat and he drew a deep shuddering breath as his hands dropped away. He took a step back. "It's becoming more than clear that you don't have to try."

Her eyes slid away and she turned away with a jerky little movement. "I'll just put the ladder back in the utility shed where I found it. I won't need it anymore today. I'm going to do some furniture polishing next."

"Furniture polishing," he repeated. He watched her in bemusement as she began to fold up the ladder. "No!" He was beside her, taking the ladder from her. "I'll take it out to the shed. You go into the parlor and sit down and rest."

"But I'm not tired. Why should I—" York wasn't listening. He was already out the screen door, carrying the ladder down the porch steps.

She frowned as she watched him cross the yard. Then she turned back to the cabinet in which she had earlier found the shelf paper. She was sure she had seen a bottle of furniture polish on the second shelf. . . .

She had finished polishing the ornate newel post at the foot of the stairs and was sitting on the third step, running the cloth over the rich oak of the rails, when he strode back into the hall. He crossed the distance between them in four strides. "I said no. Don't you ever take orders?" He took away the furniture polish and dustcloth and set them on the step. "You just left your sickbed this morning, and Deuce tells me you've already scrubbed the kitchen floor and cleaned the bathroom. Why do you think he came hotfooting it down to the mine office to get me?"

"Because he's a tattletale," she said crossly. "And because he couldn't inveigle me into another game of poker." She looked up to meet his eyes. "Is that why you decided to honor us with your presence after ignoring us for the last week? I don't need your pity, York. I don't need anyone's pity."

"If I feel any pity, it's for myself and Deuce. We don't know how to cope with pigheaded youngsters like you." His fingertips swiftly covered her lips as she started to speak. "And it *is* pigheaded. The doctor said you were to take it easy for the next month."

"He didn't say I was to be an invalid. It was only bronchitis, for heaven's sake."

"Combined with exhaustion." His lips tightened grimly. "Brady may have been willing for you to work yourself to death for him, but I'm not. You're my guest while you're here at Hell's Bluff. Accept it, Sierra."

"I can't." Her hand impulsively closed on his arm. "Don't you see I'd be perfectly miserable if I did? I have to earn my own way. I get a little panicky at even the thought of taking and not giving. I owe you too much already. I know I can't pay you back for all the trouble and medical care I've been given right now. I'll have to get a job and earn decent wages before I can begin to do that, but I can at least earn my keep until I'm strong enough to get that job." She smiled coaxingly. "And acting as housekeeper is a job that needs doing. One good housecleaning a week isn't nearly enough in a mining town like this." She paused, puzzled. "I can't understand why you sent your housekeeper away. She couldn't have been worse than putting up with a dingy house."

"Oh, no? You ought to talk to my brother Rafe sometime. Kathleen's got to be the worst housekeeper under the sun, but Deuce and I could put up with that. We've been accustomed to roughing it under a lot worse conditions. It was her cooking." He shuddered. "I had indigestion from the minute she moved in until the second she left."

Sierra smiled. In that moment, she thought, he was like an endearing little boy. "Couldn't you retire her? Deuce mentioned she was an old family retainer."

He shook his head. "That would have hurt her feelings. She and her sister, Bridget, are part of the family. They've both lived on Killara most of their adult lives. My older brother, Burke, inherited both of them when he assumed control of the business when our parents were killed in a plane crash. Bridget is the shining example of the perfect housekeeper, but Kathleen . . ."

"Night and day?" Sierra suggested with a grin.

He nodded. "Burke could stand it as long as he was spending most of his time on Killara, but when he became involved in high finance, he moved to a penthouse suite in Tucson. Bridget and Kathleen got together and decided it was only fitting that one of them should go with him. Kathleen made the supreme sacrifice, and Burke put up with her for as long as he could."

"And how did you acquire this gem?"

"When I took over the mine interests of the corporation and moved to Hell's Bluff, Burke convinced her that I needed her and shipped her off to me." He growled. "He even had the nerve to tell me it was my punishment for running wild all over the world and not assuming my proper family obligations sooner."

Sierra laughed. She couldn't help it. So even the mighty Delaney clan had their little family rifts, she thought. It was difficult to imagine the Shamrock Trinity hamstrung because of affection for an old family servant. "And you shipped her off to brother Rafe?"

"I stood it for a year," he said defensively. "It was either get her out of my kitchen or take off for South America again. I told Rafe he had a choice of accepting Kathleen or dividing his time between his precious horse ranch and tending the corporation's mining interests in Hell's Bluff."

"So why couldn't you get another housekeeper?"

"The only way I could get her to leave me without hurting her feelings was to persuade her that Rafe needed her and that it was a great sacrifice for me to give her up." His lips twisted ruefully. "I got a little carried away and told her she was irreplaceable. Now I *can't* replace her."

"Well, then you should take advantage of my being here and make use of me. I'm only temporary help, so Kathleen shouldn't mind if she should hear about it."

His gaze fell to her hand still clasping his arm. "There's only one way I'd be tempted to make use of you," he said quietly. "And we've already discussed that. You're not to do any other housework while you're on my premises, Sierra. I mean it."

"So do I." Her hand fell away from his arm. "I'm sorry, I know you only intend to be kind, but you're defeating your purpose. It will mean I have to leave your premises and find a job that much sooner."

"You'll find that hard to do in Hell's Bluff. I own this town. Give it up, Sierra," he continued softly. "When you've regained a little more of your strength, I'll send you to Tucson to Burke, and we'll find you some light clerical work to do."

"So you can continue your charity project as a family affair?" Her chin lifted. "No way, York."

He muttered something Sierra guessed was obscene. "Just look at you. So thin, a breath of wind could blow you away and shadows as deep as canyons beneath your eyes. You're already so tired, you're ready to collapse, but you won't be sensible."

"I'm not tired—" She wouldn't lie. "Well, maybe a little, since it's my first day out of bed, but I'll be fi— York!" He had risen to his feet and was pulling her to hers. "What are you doing?"

"Escorting you to your room for a nap. Forcibly if necessary." He half pushed her up the stairs. "And once there, you'll not scrub floors or wash windows. You will rest. Is that understood?"

"No, it's not understood. I'll do—" She broke off.

"Who's that? I didn't notice it when I came downstairs."

His gaze followed hers to the painting on the landing. "Rising Star."

She frowned in puzzlement. "It looks very familiar. Could I have seen it in a magazine or a gallery somewhere?"

A curious smile touched his lips as his gaze moved from the painting to Sierra's face. "No, it's never been exhibited. It's one of the family portraits from Killara. When I set up housekeeping here, Burke told me to take anything I wanted from the homestead. This was the only thing I wanted."

"Why?" she asked, looking up at him.

"I've always liked it. I used to stand and stare at it for hours when I was a boy. She was the only one of my motley crew of ancestors for whom I felt any real sense of kinship." His smile was melancholy. "Perhaps because she was as out of place at Killara as I was."

"Who was Rising Star?" she asked softly.

"The daughter of an Apache chief. Joshua Delaney took one look at her and decided he wanted her. It was during one of the powwows that took place infrequently to try to make peace between the Apaches and the Delaneys. According to legend those Delaneys were often more savage and renegade than the Indians. The Apaches were tired of fighting the Delaneys and the cavalry, too, and decided to seal the peace with a blood bond." He nodded to the portrait. "Rising Star."

"They just *gave* her to him? No wonder she looks so lost. Did she ever come to love Joshua?"

"Who knows? She had two children by him and never returned to her people. Perhaps she did love him. Or perhaps she just endured because it was her duty to honor the agreement. She looks as though she would be strong enough to endure almost anything."

"Weren't there any records? Journals, diaries?" For some reason she had an urgent desire, almost a need, to know if the woman in the portrait had ever lost that expression of loneliness and isolation.

York shook his head. "There's nothing much about Rising Star. We do know she died before Joshua and he never remarried. Neither of them kept a journal. I don't even know if Rising Star knew how to read and write."

"She would have known," Sierra said, gazing at Rising Star's serene face. "I think she would have learned everything she could, been everything she could be."

He smiled faintly. "Do you think perhaps she tried to learn one new thing every single day?"

Was he mocking her? Her gaze moved swiftly from the portrait to his face. She saw nothing there but gentleness and understanding. "It wouldn't surprise me," she said with an uncertain laugh. "I like your ancestress, York."

"So do I." He held out his hand. "And I think she'd be the first to tell you that strength should never be expended on trivial battles. Come and rest."

She stood looking at him. Such a warm smile on that beautiful face. Slowly she put her hand in his. "For today."

He nodded and started climbing the stairs, still holding her hand. "That's a start anyway. You rest this afternoon, and I'll be back this evening and see if we can't work something out."

"And how are we going to do that?" She didn't really care at the moment. His hand felt warm and caring holding her own, and he was still smiling at her with a tenderness that started a sweet trembling deep within her.

His sidewise glance was suddenly glinting with mischief. "How about a nice game of poker?"

Five

"Can we turn this off now?" York asked. "In these past few days I've had all I can stand of nighttime soap operas. *Dallas* and *Falcon Crest*, and then *Dynasty*. . . ."

Sierra's face was stricken as she turned to look at him. "Why didn't you tell me you minded?" She jumped up from the couch and ran over to turn off the television set. "You said it didn't make any difference to you what we watched. I'd never have had you sit—"

"Okay. Okay." His tone was soothing. "Don't get so upset. I didn't mind watching them." He smiled. "Though I admit I enjoyed watching you watch them more than I did the programs themselves. Your concentration fascinated me. What do you find so enthralling about them?"

She smiled uncertainly. "I suppose I do get a little absorbed. It's really not the shows themselves."

"Then what is it?"

She hesitated. For a moment she was tempted to evade answering the question. It might sound foolish, even childish, and she had never spoken of it before for that very reason. Yet York's face held no hint of mockery and his smile was gentle. She drew a deep breath. "It's because everybody in them has a place."

"A place?" he asked, puzzled.

She nodded. "I know the reason people are supposed to like those shows is because of the glitz, but I don't think that's the only reason. I watch them because it makes me feel kind of warm inside. The characters on those soaps are so assured and secure within themselves." She walked slowly toward him. Instead of sitting back down on the couch, she dropped to the floor in front of him and crossed her legs tailor-fashion. Her expression was very intent as she tried to find the words. "They have roots."

"You mean those palatial family estates?"

"Partially." She gnawed at her lower lip. "But not entirely. Having a place isn't just having a house or a family background. It's what you are inside. There's a serenity and inner confidence when you know what you are and your niche in the world." Her voice was suddenly wistful. "All my life I've wanted to have that confidence. I've always tried to make a place for myself by working and giving. I thought that was the secret, but the places I've made for myself have never lasted long. Something always happens, and I have to move on."

York's throat tightened painfully. She looked like a fragile child sitting there with her enormous dark eyes fixed so pensively on him. "You're young. Give yourself a chance."

"Maybe some people aren't meant to have a place," she whispered, almost to herself. "Maybe there's not a place for everyone." She was silent a moment, then gave herself a little half shake and straightened. "Well, I can usually find a place for myself for a little while anyway. What difference does it make if it doesn't last? There's always another chance tomorrow." She brushed a lock of hair from her temple. "You have a place, York."

"Do I?" He found his voice was a little husky. "My brothers would argue with you there. They think I have more of a tendency to wander than Johnny Appleseed did."

"Maybe you do. I guess I don't know you well enough to argue. But even if it is true, you carry your place around with you." Her smile was radiant. "And that can be pretty wonderful, you know. I wish I could."

"Why can't you?" he asked gently. "You're one of the strongest women I've ever met, Sierra. There's no reason why you shouldn't have confidence."

She shook her head. "It doesn't work that way. Oh, I'm tough all right. Lord knows I've had to be strong to fight my way out of those workers' shacks, but I still—"

"Workers' shacks?"

"My parents are migrant workers, and so are my brothers and sisters. I was born in the back of a pickup truck at the side of the road." She slowly shook her head. "My mother couldn't remember which state we were in. They had the devil of a time getting a birth certificate for me when it was time for me to start school."

"I don't know why, but I assumed you were an orphan. You seem so . . . alone."

"I am alone." She drew up her legs and linked her arms loosely about them. "I've always been alone, even when I lived with my family. There's no one more isolated than the 'different' one in the family. My parents didn't understand why I couldn't be like my brothers and sisters." She rested her chin on one knee, her lashes lowering to veil her eyes. "I couldn't accept the life we led. I didn't mind the hard labor and the traveling from state to state, but they lived without hope. I couldn't do that. I had to *try*," she said fiercely. "I studied and worked my way out of those shacks and I'm never going back. Why won't they fight? They're at the mercy of the owners, the overseers, the government, even fate itself. I wanted them to come with me, or at least let me help with the expenses to educate my youngest brother, Mark."

"They refused?"

She smiled crookedly. "Oh, they take the money I send them, but I haven't heard of any of it being spent on education. They usually buy presents for everyone in the family and spend whatever is left on parts or tires for the pickup truck." She hunched her shoulders wearily. "Maybe the presents make them happier for a little while anyway. I guess you can't force people to think as you do."

"No." He was silent for a moment, staring at her. "My Lord, you must have had a rough life."

"There were a few sharp edges." She glanced up anxiously and frowned. "Look, I'm not complaining. My childhood wasn't ideal, but whose childhood is, for heaven's sake? My parents weren't cruel, and I think they even tried to love me. They were just so beaten down, they had no energy left for affection. I've never found anyone to be really cruel once I've gotten to know and understand them. Some people can be very kind." She paused before adding gravely, "You're wonderfully kind, York."

He felt a little jolt of shock. "I don't think I've ever had anyone list kindness as one of my virtues."

"No? Then they don't really know you. You're kind and thoughtful and patient and—"

He laughed. "Are we talking about the same person? You ought to have a talk with Deuce. He knows all my faults and reminds me of them frequently."

"Yet he loves you," she said softly. "He loves you very much."

He moved his shoulders uneasily. "We've been through a lot together."

Sierra had to hide a smile when she saw that he was actually becoming embarrassed. He was incredibly lacking in conceit. It was one of the more endearing characteristics she had discovered in him. She had learned a good deal about him in the past few evenings. They had grown amazingly companionable in such a short time as they had talked, listened to music, and watched television. Besides being one of the most honest and straight-forward men she had ever met, he had a quiet sense of humor and an innate sensitivity that had surprised her. "Look how kind you've been to me," she went on. "Just the perfect example of a big brother." She grinned mischievously when she saw a slight flush rise to his cheeks. "Sorry, York. You'll simply have to get accustomed to the notion that you're absolutely wonderful."

"You're enjoying this, aren't you?" He looked at her with narrowed eyes. "You like making me uncomfortable."

"Well, I hope you noticed I refrained from mentioning you were as beautiful as a peacock again." She lowered her lashes demurely. "Though I was tempted to— York!"

He was suddenly down on the floor beside her, tumbling her backward to the carpet. He was quickly astride her, pinning her arms above her head. His sapphire eyes were laughing down at her. "A peacock, am I?"

Her own eyes were wide with surprise. She was curiously breathless, and her heart was pounding so hard, it was painful. She tried to smile and found her lips were trembling. "A very exotic peacock," she said lightly. "Why should you mind me calling you that? You must see it every time you look in the mirror." Even through the denim fabric separating them she could feel how warm his thighs were against her hips. A heated tingling was radiating from wherever his muscular legs were touching her. "Don't you?"

"Don't I what?" The laughter was gone from his eyes and they were . . . different. The pupils were dilated, and he was looking at her with an intensity that caused her to inhale sharply.

The sinewy muscles of his thighs were hardening against her soft flesh, and she felt her stomach knot, tauten, in response. There was something erotic in lying submissively beneath him like this. His lips were slightly parted, and there was a mesmerizing sensuality about them that caused her gaze to cling to them. He had asked her something, hadn't he? She couldn't gather her thoughts together to recall what it was. "I don't remember," she said.

"Neither do I." He slowly lowered his head. She couldn't look away from his beautiful mouth, and was suddenly agonizingly impatient. Why didn't he hurry? Sierra wanted to touch him, taste him. She could see the drumming of the pulse in his strong tanned throat and she wanted to touch it too. She wanted to feel that throbbing against her tongue.

He still held his body away from hers, though he was close enough for her to feel its heat reach out and enfold her. "Tilt back your head, Sierra."

She obeyed eagerly, instinctively. "I love your neck," he murmured. "The skin is so soft, like velvet. I've wanted to . . ." His lips touched the sensitive cord at the side of her neck, and she gasped.

He was kissing her tenderly, lovingly, little kisses

that drifted over her from the soft underside of her jaw to the hollow of her shoulder. Soft and sweet, yet each one sent a slow stream of fire into her veins. She moved her head from side to side, trying to offer more of herself to him. She arched her spine, desperate to touch him, to bring him closer, and her breasts brushed against his chest.

He shuddered and froze into stillness. "Do that again," he said hoarsely.

She wanted it too. She wanted to feel his firm muscles against her softness. Yet she wasn't really soft now, she noticed. Her breasts were swollen and heavy, the nipples pointing boldly through the fabric of her T-shirt. She lifted her body mindlessly, helplessly, rubbing against him with a pleasure that was near to pain. "York, this is . . ."

His eyes were closed, and he began to move his hips against her with the same heedless compulsion that was driving her. "Shhh. It'll be all right. Just let me . . ."

She could feel the iron-hard length of him pushing against her, and she bit her lip to keep back the low moan that was trembling in her throat. Empty. She was so empty and yearning and . . .

His eyes flicked open. They were glazed and seemed almost blind with need. "Sierra, I have to have you. I'm hurting so damn much—" He suddenly broke off and drew a deep breath. "Lord, what am I saying?" Every muscle in his body seemed unbearably taut. Then he released her arms and swung off her with a lack of coordination that made him appear clumsy. His chest was still heaving with his labored breathing as he rose to his feet. "Come on. Get up," he said.

She sat up a little dazedly. What had happened? He had left her so abruptly, tearing and destroying the lovely web of sensuality she hadn't even known they were weaving.

"Get up and go to your room." His hands were clenched at his sides. "I'm sorry I can't act the gentleman and help you up, but I can't afford to touch you right now."

"All right." She stood up, It had happened so swiftly, she was still bewildered. She hadn't realized that levity could change to desire in the flicker of a moment. She turned quickly to the door. She wanted to leave as much as he wanted her to go. She had to think and try to get everything into perspective.

"Sierra."

She tensed. "Yes."

"I've never felt like a big brother toward you. Don't make that mistake again."

"No." She moistened her lips with her tongue. "No, I won't."

Her steps were so swift, she was almost running as she left the parlor.

The music playing on the stereo was as soothing as a Brahms lullaby, Sierra thought crossly. Maybe it was Brahms. The choice would have been on a par with the rest of York's behavior this evening. He had been just as soothing and remote. She had been conscious of the tension behind his polite mask since he had walked through the front door tonight. After dinner he had hustled her into the parlor, put the record on, and retired immediately to the library.

It shouldn't have hurt. She had no right to be hurt, she assured herself as she took the one record off and put on Ravel's *Bolero* instead. She had been spoiled these last few days when York had spent each evening with her. It had been foolish to believe he had enjoyed their time together as much as she had. Probably, he had merely been indulging her as he would a restless, fractious child. After last night he had no doubt decided they'd come too close to an unwanted intimacy and was trying to set a certain distance between them.

"What on earth has that poor machine done to you?" She turned to see Deuce standing in the doorway, a large glass of orange juice in his hand. "Judging by the scowl on your face I'd say you were about to take a hatchet to it."

She smiled with an effort. "Destroy a state-of-the-art stero? Not likely. I'd be in debt for the next ten years if I did." She slid the record York had chosen back into its jacket and saw it was, indeed, Brahms. "It was the music I objected to, not the equipment. York evidently decided Brahms would be just the ticket to keep me calm and complacent this evening. I've decided I hate Brahms."

"I'm not overfond of him myself." Deuce walked across the room to her. "A bit heavy for my taste."

"Boring," she said curtly.

"York wants you to drink this." He held out the glass of orange juice. "I took him some coffee and he said to make sure you had your vitamin C as well as your iron tablets before you went to bed."

So York didn't intend to leave the library again tonight, she thought. She quickly smothered a pang of disappointment as she took the glass. "Thank you. I won't forget, but I'm not ready to go to bed yet. I'm a little too restless to settle down for the night."

"I noticed. Ravel instead of Brahms. Strange, York should make that selection. I had the distinct impression he, too, was more in the mood for Ravel tonight."

"Evidently you were wrong." She took a sip of the orange juice. "Or maybe he thinks Brahms is as therapeutic as vitamin C for pitiful little invalids like yours truly."

"Do I detect a trace of sarcasm?"

"Sorry. I guess I'm feeling a little smothered at the moment." She sipped some more juice, then set the glass on a table. "I'm not used to all this lolling around with no work to do. To tell you the truth, I have a bad case of cabin fever."

"Really?" He lifted a brow. "I thought you were settling down quite nicely the last few days."

"Appearances can deceive." She turned to the door. "I think I'll go for a little stroll before I turn in. I haven't been out of the house since I've been ill, and I was too busy to go sight-seeing when I was with the troupe. I don't even know what Hell's Bluff looks like."

"Wouldn't it be wiser to wait until daylight? You can't see much at night."

She shook her head. "I won't go far."

"All right, I'll go with you."

"No." It came out sharper than she meant, and she smiled apologetically. "You'd better let me go alone. I'm afraid I wouldn't be good company at the moment. My nerves are a little on edge. I won't be gone long."

"Whatever you say," Deuce said, shrugging. "You'd better run upstairs and get a jacket. It may be April, but it's still damn cold here in the mountains."

She nodded with relief. She had thought Deuce would be more difficult to discourage. "I'll do that, and I'll be sure to take my pills when I get back. I'm not stupid enough to risk getting sick again. I know I've been enough trouble as it is." She started across the room. "I'll see you later, Deuce."

He watched her as she climbed the stairs, then turned and walked quickly down the hall to the library. York looked up as the door opened.

"Orange juice delivered," Deuce said. "And she's

promised faithfully to take her pills." He paused. "Just as soon as she gets back."

"Back? Where the hell is she going?"

"Just for a walk. She says she has cabin fever."

"Go with her," York said tersely. "You know it's not safe for her to wander around here alone."

"She didn't want my company. Shall I call one of the men and tell him to follow and make sure she's safe?"

"He'd probably scare her to death creeping along behind her. Why the devil didn't you insist, dammit?"

"Because I knew she wouldn't listen, and I detest useless effort," Deuce drawled. "She's as edgy as you are tonight and probably for the same reason."

York gazed at him coolly. "And what is that?"

"I also detest stating the obvious, but I will in this case." Deuce steadily returned his stare. "You need to spend an hour or two at Melanie's. You're horny as hell. I think you're lusting after our little Sierra."

"Well, that's blunt enough," York said dryly. He looked away. "I told you, I don't have a thing for wide-eyed waifs."

"But you have a thing for Sierra Smith," Deuce said softly. "Waif or not, you have a big yen for the lady. I've known you long enough to realize what's going on here. I can also see that you're not going to do anything about it. Go to Melanie's, York."

York was silent as conflicting emotions battled within him. "If you remember, I went to Melanie's every night last week. I had something of that nature in mind myself." He suddenly sounded weary. "It didn't do any good."

Deuce raised a brow. "No?"

"No." York's laugh had an edge of frustration. "I didn't want any of them. I had my dinner and a drink and came home." His voice lowered. "I don't want anyone but her. Idiotic, isn't it?"

Deuce hesitated. "She's a nice young woman, York. I like her."

"So do I, dammit," he said with a touch of leashed violence. "Why do you think I'm going through this hell? You know I'd probably make her miserable. I'd make any woman miserable."

"Probably," Deuce agreed.

"You're nothing if not frank." York's lips twisted into a cynical smile. "I can always rely on you to attest to the wickedness of my character."

"You know better than that. You're a damn fine friend, and I don't know anyone I'd rather have in my corner." Deuce slowly shook his head. "But, as my dear old gin-soaked mum used to say to me, 'Yer just not steady, me lad.' " His expression was suddenly serious. "I think Sierra is the type of person who needs someone who's steady as a rock. She's had enough uncertainty in her life."

"So what do I do? I can't send her away, or she'll find a way to work herself into a relapse. I can't keep her here or—as sure as hell—we'll end up in bed together."

"That is a problem." Deuce walked over to an easy chair and dropped into it with loose-boned grace. "But I wouldn't count on the decision being entirely yours to make. Sierra has a mind of her own, and she's not exactly predictable." He tilted his head, listening. "I think I just heard the front door slam. Are you going after her?"

York pushed his chair back almost violently. "Hell yes, I'm going after her. With her facility for trouble she'll probably fall down a mine shaft." He started for the door. "Are you coming?"

Deuce shook his head and leaned back in his chair. "I've said my piece. I now intend to be discreet and sit back and let nature take its course. Not that it wouldn't anyway."

York cursed as he flung the door open.

"York, there's something else you should know."

York glanced over his shoulder impatiently. "What?"

"Sierra hates Brahms."

This time the muttered imprecation was a good deal more obscene, and Deuce smiled with enjoyment as York strode out of the room.

"Wait!"

The command was so clipped and edged with irritation that Sierra stopped short. York? She turned to see him walking down the street toward her, quickly jerking on his sheepskin jacket. Her heart lifted with eagerness, then fell immediately when she saw the scowl on his face. She smiled tentatively as he came abreast of her.

"You decided you needed some air too?" she asked.

"No, I decided I didn't want to strangle some bastard who might decide to rape you." He grasped her elbow and began to walk, half dragging her down the street. "You wanted to sightsee? Let's go."

"You're angry." She had to hurry to keep up. "I didn't mean for Deuce to bother you. Please go back to your work. I'll be fine by myself."

"This is a town with no women. Do I need to remind you of that fact? Even if you were the drab nonentity you think you are, you'd attract attention here. There are close to a thousand men in Hell's Bluff who would like nothing better than to haul you off to bed."

She halted abruptly and jerked her arm out of his grasp. "All right, let's go back," she said quietly. "You had only to tell me that. I don't want to cause any more trouble. I know how much I owe you."

"You don't owe me—" He broke off as he looked down at her. Her eyes held hurt as well as the strength and dignity that was so much a part of her. He felt his anger melting away like snow in the spring as that familiar, tender yearning filled him. "Look, I'm sorry. I'm acting like an autocratic idiot. You have a perfect right to go for a walk, but this just isn't the kind of town to take a casual stroll in. Some of these miners are steady family men. But some are rough enough not to care if you're under my protection if they decide they want a roll in the hay."

"I'll remember that. I'll go back now." She started to turn around and was stopped by his hand on her arm.

"No, we might as well go a little farther now that we're here. What did you want to see?" He was smiling down at her with surprising gentleness. "It's a very small town, and it won't take long. This particular side of Hell's Bluff is practically deserted anyway."

"Why?" She gazed around with interest. The wooden sidewalk on which they were standing was a good foot off the hard-packed dirt of the street. Over the sidewalk was a wooden awning that would shelter pedestrians from rain and snow. The shops and restaurants they had passed were locked and dark, and she wondered about that. "Chester said you had restored the entire town," she said.

"I did, but these stores aren't necessary to the actual running of the mine, so I've never staffed them. When the ore runs out, we'll probably open the town up as a tourist attraction, and then this area will be in full operation."

"Is the ore about to run out?"

He shrugged. "Not for years. This is a very rich deposit, but you always have to be ready for the next step."

She studied him in the moonlight. "But I don't think that's why you had the town restored. I believe you would have done it anyway."

"Maybe I would have at that. I feel more comfortable in surroundings like these. Boom towns are here today and gone tomorrow." He paused. "Like me, Sierra."

She ran her tongue over her lower lip. "That sounds remarkably like a warning. You seem to be handing out quite a few of those these days. I can't imagine why. I'm perfectly able to take care of myself."

"I'm glad one of us is confident. I've had a few misgivings about my own ability to handle the situation." He smiled faintly. "You have a very odd effect upon me, Sierra Smith."

"I don't mean to make you uncomfortable," she said hurriedly. "This is your home and I'd never want to—"

His fingers covered her lips, stopping the flow of words. "Hush," he said gently. "I know that. You're falling all over yourself to keep from causing any trouble."

His fingertips were tracing her soft lips, and she could feel a throbbing sensitivity wherever he touched her. He must be able to feel that throbbing beneath his fingers, she thought. It was vibrating through her entire body, making her tremble helplessly. "I don't think you should be doing this."

"I don't either. I shouldn't have touched you. I wasn't going to do that. I knew—" He broke off. "Oh, Lord, come *here.*"

She was in his arms and his mouth was covering hers with a hard passion. He stole her breath and ignited a raging fire between her thighs. His tongue slipped between her parted lips and caressed hers. An undeniable yearning built inside her, and it was impossible not to return his hot kiss with equal passion.

She made a sound deep in her throat and arched up against him as if he had pulled a string connected to every muscle in her body. He was trembling against her, his chest rising and falling rapidly with the force of his breathing. He lifted his head slightly, but his tongue still moved against her lips between his whispered words.

"I've wanted to do this every minute for the last three days. I've wanted my tongue on you, and my hands . . ." His hands slipped down to cup the curve of her bottom. "And my . . ."

With a sudden forceful movement he lifted her and held her against the cradle of his hips. She gasped as she felt the hardness of his arousal through the flimsy barriers of cloth that separated them.

"Here too," he said thickly. "I need all of you. I need to come into you and—" He stopped and drew a deep breath. "I can't even talk, dammit. But I can show you."

He pulled her into the dark alcove of a shop entry and pressed her against the wall. He flipped open her coat with swift rough hands and pulled the T-shirt out of her jeans. "I want to see you," he said jerkily. "Not that I can see much in these shadows." He was impatiently pushing up the T-shirt. "Is it all right?"

"Yes." She wanted to see him too. He was so beautiful. She wished she could see his eyes as he was looking at her.

He was loosening her bra, and then his hands were on her breasts, enveloping their smallness in his palms. The feel of his hard calloused hands on her bare skin sent a shocking, burning sensation through her. She gave a broken little cry and surged toward him.

"It's not enough," he muttered. "I can't *see* you." His hands were squeezing and caressing with a rhythm that caused her breath to catch in her throat. "I want you to be open to me. I want . . ." The rest of his sentence was lost as his mouth enveloped one aching, swollen breast.

His tongue flicked the sensitive nipple and she had to grit her teeth to keep from crying out. His hand moved down between her thighs and began rubbing against her with slow, lazy strokes while his lips suckled with increasing force. The denim of her jeans might just as well have not been there. She felt as if he were stroking her naked flesh, and her legs became so weak, she had to lean back against the wall for support. She gasped for breath. The tugging at her nipple was causing her stomach to knot painfully, and his hand . . .

"You like that?" he asked, lifting his head. He caressed her breast with his free hand and chuckled huskily. "Yes, I can see you do." His hand between her thighs suddenly closed and tightened. She gasped and a shudder ran through her. "And you like that too. It's going to be a joy finding all the things that pleasure you, Sierra." His hands were leaving her. He adjusted her bra and pulled down her shirt. "And I'm going to enjoy every minute of it." He pulled her out onto the sidewalk.

The moonlight was dawn-bright in comparison to the alcove's deep shadows. York looked down at Sierra and saw she was gazing up at him. Her dark eyes were shining with an eagerness and a breathless joy, and his heart turned over as tenderness returned tenfold. He felt it flow over him, sparking a foreign aching deep within. "Don't do this to me," he said hoarsely. "I don't want to feel like this."

"Like what?" She scarcely realized what she had said. He was looking down at her with those deep blue eyes that held beauty and kindness and—

"As if I've come loose from my moorings and drifted out to sea." He touched her cheek gently, and a glowing warmth drifted through her. "Every time I look at you, I get a little closer to the point of no return."

"I thought that was airplanes, not ships," she said breathlessly. "You're getting your metaphors mixed." His fingers were burning against her cheek, and her heart was beating so crazily, she was sure he could hear it. It was she who was lost in the sea of emotion. He must have experienced at least a facsimile of this turbulence before. "Not that it matters."

"No, not that it matters," he agreed. His fingers moved to her kiss-swollen lips and pressed softly against them. "This is the only thing that matters. Let's go back to the house, Sierra."

"Yes." She was vaguely aware he was turning, his hand on her waist gently propelling her the short block back to the house. His fingers ran from her elbow down to her hand and caught it in a warm strong grasp. She felt a tiny thrill as her hand curled instinctively around his. "All this feels so . . ." Her voice trailed off. They had reached the front porch, and the garish red light was casting a rosy glow over the beautiful tautness of York's cheekbones. He was going to make love to her. The knowledge sent a wild excitement through every vein. She could see the burning intensity in his eyes. He *wanted* her. This wonderful, kind, beautiful man wanted her. "We're going to go to bed together," she said. It was a statement not a question.

"If I can hold on that long. If we don't hurry, we may not leave this porch."

"I'm not very experienced," she said gravely. "I think you should know that. But I'll try very hard, and that will count for something, won't it?"

Why did everything she say invoke this terrible tenderness that made his eyes sting and his throat tighten helplessly? he wondered. "That will count for a hell of a lot." He drew her into his arms and pressed her close. She was so delicate. He felt he could break her with just the pressure of his hands. The tenderness was still there, but his body was hardening, readying. The muscles of his stomach tightened with the same hunger he had known only a few minutes before. "You always try hard, don't you? You give everything that's in you."

His lips were just above hers, and he could see their trembling vulnerability. York had a sudden desire to crush, to bruise, to tear at that vulnerability. The thought sent a chilling shock through him. What the hell was wrong with him? The impulse had been as savagely primitive as his other reactions toward Sierra. He had never wanted to be rough with any woman. Why did Sierra have this effect on him? he asked himself.

Because he didn't want her to remain vulnerable.

The answer exploded inside him. He wanted to destroy that part of her so he could take and still be free to walk away. Good Lord, what kind of monster was he?

"What's wrong?" she asked, seeing the different expressions chase across his face. "Did I say something wrong?"

He pushed her away with scarcely contained violence. "You sure as hell did. You said yes, dammit. Don't you have any sense of self-preservation? I told you an affair with me wouldn't be safe for you."

Her bewilderment turned to pain. "You don't want me anymore?" She drew a shaky breath and lifted her chin. "I understand. It was an impulse, right? You mustn't think you have to pretend—"

"Pretend! Lord, don't you have ears? I want you so much, I'm aching for it. I want you so much, I can't be in the same room with you without wanting to reach out and grab." He drew a rasping breath and his eyes blazed down at her. "You're making my life miserable as hell. I wish to God you'd never come to this town."

She backed away from him, her face white and stricken. "I'm sorry." Oh, Lord, she thought. She was stammering a little. She mustn't do that. It was this damn pain. She tried to make her voice firm. "I know I've been a burden to you in all sorts of ways. I didn't mean to be—" Her voice broke and she had to stop.

"Damn." York's voice was harsh with remorse. He saw her pained expression, highlighted by the glare of the red lantern. He stepped forward impulsively. "Sierra, I didn't mean—"

"Don't touch me." She backed away from him. "I know you didn't want to hurt me. You don't have to tell me that. For heaven's sake, don't *pity* me."

She jerked open the door and ran inside. Her eyes were so blinded by tears that she almost collided with Deuce as she tore up the stairs toward the haven of her room. She muttered something she hoped was an apology as she took the steps two at a time.

"Sierra!" York called after her. "I didn't want—"

She didn't stop. She couldn't bear to face him right now. Not until the first agony of the pain of rejection was over. She'd be all right then. She'd faced rejection before. But York's rejection hurt so much worse than the others. She slammed her bedroom door behind her.

Deuce flinched at the sound. "Perhaps I should have been the one to go after her," he said to York.

"You don't seem to be handling Sierra with your usual finesse."

York laughed harshly. "That's certainly putting it conservatively. There's nothing in the least usual about my relationship with Sierra. I can't seem to open my mouth without hurting her."

Deuce gazed at him steadily. "Better a little pain now than a basketful later. Get rid of her, York. You're going to hurt her badly, and you're not hard enough to do that without hurting yourself too."

York was well aware of that. When he'd seen the torment on Sierra's face, he had felt her pain as if it were his own. He had wanted to take her in his arms and hold and rock her as if she were a hurt child. But she wasn't a child, and if she stayed here he was going to be the one who hurt her. He didn't want to do that.

"You're right," he said wearily as he shrugged out of his coat. "She can't stay here any longer. I'll have to work something out, and heaven only knows what that will be. I can't send her away without someone to look after her." He tossed his coat in the direction of the cushioned bench against the wall and turned toward the library. "I have a few phone calls to make. Why don't you get that bottle of Napoleon brandy you won from the owner of that silver mine in Ixtapa? I'm going to need something very smooth, potent, and alcoholic to wash this particular experience away."

"Okay, if you think it will help."

York had a very good idea that it wouldn't help at all, but he'd try anything to forget Sierra's eyes filled with bewilderment and pain. "Just bring it, will you?"

"How is she?" York asked Deuce the next evening. He glanced up the stairs and tried to keep the tenseness out of his voice. "Did she eat anything today? She didn't come down to breakfast this morning."

Deuce shrugged. "She ate a little lunch. As for her mental state, it's not all that good. I don't know what you said to her last night, but it took all the juice out of her. She's been floating around here all day as lackluster as a ghost, except for that walk she took into town this afternoon. Are you going to try to talk to her? I believe an apology must definitely be in order," he added pointedly.

"Get off my back, Deuce." York rubbed his neck wearily. "I know the effect she must have had on you today. I'd probably be ready to bust a few faces myself if I'd had to see her hurting, but I'm not up to any needling at the moment."

"But you didn't have to see her," Deuce said dryly. "You ran off to the office and left it to me. I didn't like that, York. If you're going to scatter carnage, you should be there to tidy up later."

Carnage. The word made York flinch. It reminded him too vividly of Sierra's expression under the glare of those red porch lights. "That's what I'm trying to do," he said. "Just hold the fort for another few hours while I bring in reinforcements."

"Reinforcements?"

York looked at his watch. "I'm going to the heliport right now to pick up Rafe and Burke."

"So those were the calls you made last night. You must be in dire straits if you sent out an S.O.S. I've never known you to ask them for help before," he said thoughtfully.

"Only because they lavished so much help on me when I was a kid that I nearly smothered in it," York said with a touch of grimness. "I swore a long time ago no one was ever going to fight my battles again."

Deuce stared speculatively at York. "Until now."

"Until now." York turned away with an abrupt, almost savage, movement. "Keep a watch over her until I get back. With any luck that responsibility won't be ours after tomorrow."

"I'll do that." Deuce paused. "You know, I think I'm going to miss this particular responsibility. Sierra has a way of growing on you."

"I will too." York kept his face averted as he opened the front door. He could feel the loneliness already, and she hadn't even left Hell's Bluff yet, he thought. This morning at breakfast he'd had the first inkling of how much she had insinuated her way into his life in the past few weeks. It had seemed wrong to sit there without her across from him with her sudden glowing smile and dark eyes . . . His hand tightened on the doorknob as he remembered how her eyes had looked last night. "Do me a favor, Deuce? Get someone to change those red light bulbs on the porch to white before I get back. I'm tired of that red glow."

"Really? I thought the concept amused you."

He saw again Sierra's thin face illuminated by the harsh scarlet, her lips trembling with pain.

"It doesn't amuse me any longer. I'm sick to death of it. Have the bulbs changed." He slammed the door behind him.

The sun was going down behind the mountains as Rafe's helicopter, with the official Shamrock logo on its side, descended to the concrete Tarmac. Rafe had scarcely time to jump from the craft and start toward where York was standing beside the Jeep when Burke's identical helicopter began to descend.

Rafe halted and waited for Burke to join him, then they walked together toward York. York could hear Burke's deep murmur and Rafe's easy laugh. It was all so familiar, he felt as if he were a boy again on Killara. How many times had he watched a much younger Burke and Rafe join in the warm camraderie he had envied with everything in him? For a moment he felt again the sharp, aching pain of isolation, then it was gone. What stupid tricks memory played, he thought.

He stepped forward and was immediately enfolded in the bond of love and togetherness. It had always been there waiting for him. All he'd ever had to do was step forward. It had taken him a hell of a long time to learn that.

"This had better be damn important, brother mine," Burke said. "I had to drop a very delicate transaction to answer this particular mayday."

"Another merger?" York asked idly as he shook hands.

Burke's smile was almost grim. "In a manner of speaking."

"What do we need with another merger?" Rafe asked. He stepped into the back of the Jeep and stretched his long legs out as far as the shallow confines would permit. "I would think the only company we haven't merged with or taken over is IBM."

"No, that's next month," Burke said, deadpan. "Providing I can fit it into my schedule." He climbed into the front passenger seat. "Don't worry, neither one of you are going to be bothered with the details of this merger. It's strictly private stock, and I intend to keep it that way."

"For which York and I will breathe a profound sigh of relief," Rafe drawled. "You may enjoy these convoluted maneuvers, but we'd rather just get on with day-to-day earthy practicalities." He frowned as a thought struck him. "You're not supposed to be taking on any new projects right now, Burke. You've worn yourself to a frazzle lately trying to run the corporation and fight that shyster in court."

"This transaction has a few fringe benefits I

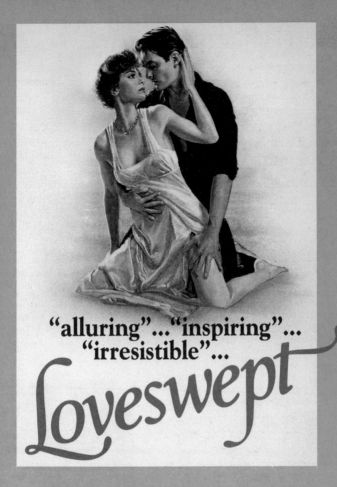

"alluring"... "inspiring"...
"irresistible"...

Loveswept

EXAMINE 4 LOVESWEPT NOVELS FOR

15 Days FREE!

Turn page for details

America's most popular, most compelling romance novels...

Loveswept

Here, at last...love stories that really involve you! Fresh, finely crafted novels with story lines so believable you'll feel you're actually living them!

Read a Loveswept novel and you'll experience all the very real feelings of two people as they discover and build an involved relationship: laughing, crying, learning and loving. Characters you can relate to... exciting places to visit...unexpected plot twists...all in all, exciting romances that satisfy your mind and delight your heart.

And now you can be sure you'll never, ever miss a single Loveswept title by enrolling in our special reader's home delivery service. A service that will bring all four new Loveswept romances published every month into your home—and deliver them to you *before* they appear in the bookstores!

Examine 4 Loveswept Novels for

15 Days FREE!

To introduce you to this fabulous service, you'll get four brand-new Loveswept releases not yet in the bookstores. These four exciting new titles are yours to examine for 15 days without obligation to buy. Keep them if you wish for just $9.95 plus postage and handling and any applicable sales tax.

SEND NO MONEY NOW.
RETURN THIS
POSTAGE-PAID CARD TODAY!

BUSINESS REPLY MAIL

FIRST-CLASS MAIL   PERMIT NO. 2456   HICKSVILLE, NY

Postage will be paid by addressee

Loveswept

Bantam Books
P.O. Box 985
Hicksville, NY 11802

couldn't resist." Burke gestured impatiently with his hand. "Drop it, Rafe. I'm not that tired, and that's not why we're here. It's York who has the problem." He turned in his seat as York started the Jeep. "So let's get your difficulty out on the table and find a solution for it. What is it? Labor? Or has that damn import policy been hamstringing you?"

"Neither one." York shifted uneasily in his seat and pressed his foot down with unconscious force on the accelerator. "It's personal, not business."

"Personal?" Rafe stiffened and stared with concern at York. "Is the grass beginning to look greener somewhere else? You're probably just bored. Come down to my place next week and"—he hesitated before finishing lamely—"well, on second thought maybe you'd better wait a week or so. There's a horse I may have to go take a look at fairly soon, and I wouldn't be able to devote any time to you until—"

"Rafe," York interrupted, "if you'll stop trying to save me from myself, I'll tell you what the problem is." The glance he gave Rafe over his shoulder held both exasperation as well as affection. "You needn't rearrange your schedule or find the time to brainwash me on the glories of the settled and sedate life. Not that you've ever been a prime example of either of those qualities."

Rafe's gypsy dark eyes were suddenly dancing. "I had to keep up with you, and Burke, didn't I? The youngest always carries that psychological burden."

"If I remember, I was the one who always came in last," York said with a faint touch of irony.

Burke's smile was surprisingly gentle in his rough-hewn face. "That's not true. Just the fact that you entered the race at all assured you of first place."

"So you always told me," York said. "I never

believed you, but it made me feel better at the time." His tension was beginning to ebb marginally as Rafe and Burke's presence worked their usual magic. When the three men were together, he had always felt stronger, surer, and more capable of handling anything—even the phantom that had dogged his childhood. "In a way I'm still running a race against time. I was hoping you could help me."

"Name it," Burke said.

"We'll work it out." Rafe's smile was reassuring.

York took a deep breath. "It's a woman."

Burke's usually impassive face showed a flicker of surprise. "My problem?"

"A bogus paternity suit?" York shook his head. "No way."

Rafe was chuckling. "A woman. You have to be kidding. There hasn't been a woman you couldn't lure into your bed since you were thirteen."

"I don't want to lure her into my bed," York said from between clenched teeth. "I'm trying to keep her out of it. And it's not funny, Rafe."

Rafe's smile instantly disappeared. "So tell us about it."

York did just that, as clearly and unemotionally as possible.

By the time he had finished, Rafe was laughing again. As York gave him a far-from-pleasant glance his younger brother held up his hand in protest. "I'm not laughing at you. I swear it on old Shamus's grave. I was just thinking it never rains but it pours." He suddenly looked thoughtfully at Burke. "And I was wondering if that maxim would apply to your little merger."

"Stop being cryptic, Rafe," Burke said. "Suppose we address York's problem?"

Rafe grinned. "Whatever you say, big brother." He leaned forward and rested his arms on the back of Burke's seat. "I'll be delighted to lend my invaluable insight as soon as York tells us what he wants us to do."

"I want one of you to take her home with you tomorrow when you leave," York said, not looking at either of them. "She won't be any trouble; she's an appealing scamp. You'll like her."

Neither Rafe nor Burke answered.

York's hands tightened on the wheel. "For Pete's sake, I'm not asking you to adopt her. I just want you to take her in for a few months until she's well again."

"Let's clarify this a little, shall we?" Burke said frowning. "You're not just asking for a home and keep for the girl. You'd want us to actually take her under our wing and keep an eye on her personally?"

York nodded. "She needs looking after, and you're the only people I'd trust to do it right."

Burke swore beneath his breath. "It's the wrong *time*, York. Why couldn't you have asked this a month ago?"

"Because I'd never heard of Sierra Smith a month ago," York said. "Your merger is that urgent?"

Burke grimaced. "More urgent every day."

York half turned. "Rafe?"

Rafe slowly shook his head. "Not if there's any other way. Your Sierra sounds as if she's going to require more attention than I can give her right now. I think you're going to have to work this one out for yourself, York."

"I told you how it would end up if I didn't get her out of Hell's Bluff. She's not like anyone else I've ever met. She feels more intensely. She'd be—" York stopped abruptly. He had sounded almost desperate. It wasn't Rafe's or Burke's fault he had chosen an awkward time for both of them. How would he have felt if someone had tried to thrust a strange woman on him? Yet if he had met Sierra and realized how sweet and strong and brave she was, he would have taken her. He wouldn't have been able to help himself, no matter how it disrupted his life-style. Perhaps Sierra would have the same effect on Burke and Rafe once they got to know her. She'd certainly managed to wrap Deuce around her finger in the short time she'd been at Hell's Bluff. "We'll talk about it later," he said as he braked on the rock driveway beside the house. "Meet Sierra first."

"I can't wait to do just that," Rafe drawled as he jumped lithely from the Jeep. "I trust you didn't take in the python too? That would have been really fascinating."

"No python," York said with a grin. He stepped out of the Jeep, then waited until Burke and Rafe joined him on the brick walkway leading around to the front porch. "I would have had to get rid of Deuce if I'd brought Bathsheba home."

"How is Deuce?" Burke paused. He reached the front porch and a frown creased his brow. "There's something different . . ." His gaze flicked to York. "Where are the infamous red lights? I almost didn't recognize your front porch."

York shrugged. "I decided it was too predictable a touch, so I got rid of them."

"Interesting," Rafe murmured.

Burke made no comment, but there was a curiously thoughtful expression on his face as he followed York into the house.

"Take off your coats and go into the library," York said as he strode toward the kitchen. "I'll hunt up Deuce, and we'll have a drink before dinner."

He appeared in the library a few minutes later. "I can't find him," he said, puzzled. "He wouldn't have gone out. I told him to stick around and take care of Sierra."

"That appears to be your injunction to everyone

these days," Burke said dryly. "There's a note on the mantel over there." He nodded to the fireplace across the room. "Deuce?"

York's frown faded as he recognized Deuce's beautifully scrolled handwriting on the envelope. "Deuce," he confirmed as he pulled out the single sheet of paper. "I wonder what the hell he's up— Dammit" His hand tightened on the note until his knuckles showed white. He felt as if his insides had blown apart.

"York?" Rafe was instantly beside him, his voice filled with concern. "What is it?"

"What do you think it is?" York's own voice was suddenly savage as he crushed the paper. "It's Sierra. Who else is turning my life inside out? She decided not to wait for me to dispose of her to suit myself. I should have known she wouldn't, dammit. Sierra's always the one to take the initiative."

"Calm down, York," Burke said quietly. "Tell us what's happened. What do you mean, she's taken the initiative?"

York dropped the ball of paper on the floor and turned toward the door. "She packed up and slipped out of the house. Deuce took off after her as soon as he read the note she left in her room. Apparently it was a very polite note, saying thank you and telling us where she was going so we wouldn't worry." He laughed mirthlessly. "Worry! My Lord, why shouldn't we worry?"

"Where has she gone?" Rafe asked as he picked up his coat and started after York. "I gather we're going in pursuit?"

"You're damn right we are," York said grimly. "Sierra went out and got herself a job this afternoon. She's now working for Melanie Dolan at the Soiled Dove."

Six

Melanie Dolan's usually serene expression was marred by a frown. "I'm not at all sure I'm not being an idiot to even try this," she said to Sierra. "It's not a good idea to confuse the customers. A house is either one thing or the other."

"I'll be very clear about making sure the men know I'm just a waitress and not one of your girls," Sierra said earnestly. "I've been a waitress before and I'm very good at it. You won't be disappointed, Melanie."

"It's not my disappointment I'm worried about. Some of my customers aren't gentlemen enough to take a flat no without an argument." She shrugged. "Well, I promised you a trial night and I'll stick to it." She pushed back the gray leather executive chair and rose gracefully to her feet.

Melanie Dolan was a wildly improbable anomaly in the cool businesslike atmosphere of the room, Sierra thought. There was an IBM computer on her desk and steel file cabinets across the room, sleekly decorated in blue and gray. In contrast Melanie herself was all warmth and provocative, lush sensuality. Her shoulder-length auburn hair had been cut by a master hand to frame her classic features and the vibrant color flamed above the ice-blue lamé gown lovingly hugging her curvaceous figure. She looked alluring, sexy, and totally in control. However, her quiet assurance did nothing to diminish the warmth of her smile or the humor flickering in those velvet brown eyes.

Melanie stepped around the desk and paused before Sierra. "Come along downstairs and I'll introduce you to the bartender. It sounds as if things are beginning to liven up." She smoothed back one of the dark silky wisps of hair that framed Sierra's face and shook her head. "It's a mistake. Why the hell am I doing this?"

Sierra smiled brightly. "Because you're a very nice person and a good businesswoman. And because you know I'll give good value for my wages."

Melanie arched a brow. "Oh, is that my motivation? I'm glad you explained. I've been wondering ever since I let you talk me into this." She opened the door to her office and gestured for Sierra to precede her. "Let's just see how good a businesswoman I am. Welcome to the Dove, Sierra."

Sierra drew a deep breath and kept a confident smile fixed firmly on her face as she sailed through the door. As she walked, her full taffeta skirts rustled with a slight sensual hiss. The short emerald-green gown itself was sensual, which hadn't occurred to her when Melanie had given it to her to alter this afternoon. Though the gown's cut was simple, the color was eye-catching and gave her pale matte complexion a glow. The off-the-shoulder neckline and tight waist and bodice reminded her of a dance-hall girl's costume in an old John Wayne movie. Oh, well, why was she worrying? After all, she did try to learn something new every day; maybe this would be a good opportunity. And, besides, sensuous gown or not, she couldn't hold a candle to red-haired Melanie or her girls when it came to sexiness. No one would look twice at her with all those exotic birds of paradise floating around the barroom.

Birds of paradise. She wished she hadn't thought of that comparison. The simile reminded her of that afternoon in the kitchen when York . . . No, she mustn't think of York or anything but the job she had to do.

The noise, the smoke, and the odor of beer struck her as soon as she left the office. From where she stood on the second floor she could look down on the barroom itself. Again she was reminded of a Wild West movie.

Melanie Dolan had done a superb job of creating an atmosphere to fit in with the town. The hallway on the second floor formed a U-shaped balcony that surrounded the bar on three sides. Private rooms opened off the hall. A staircase, carpeted in the same plum shade as the hall, led down to the first floor. The barroom was dominated by an enormous, magnificent bar. Over it hung an equally enormous painting of a plump reclining nude with several white doves fluttering around her.

"Gloriously tacky, huh?" Melanie said, following Sierra's gaze to the painting. "But York wanted authenticity, and it certainly is that. How do you like Bertha and Charlie?"

"Bertha and Charlie?"

Melanie gestured to the other side of the room, where a giant swing was suspended from the ceiling by two braided silver cords. Two white plaster of Paris doves at least three feet high were nestling coyly on the bar of the swing.

"My doves," Melanie said. "I figured after the nauseating tackiness of the painting, there was no place to go but up. I really wanted a red velvet swing à la the Floradora Girls, but I knew, sure as shooting, one of the customers would find a way of getting one of my girls up there on the swing." She made a face. "So I settled for Bertha and Charlie and the bird swing."

Frankly Sierra thought the swing was even tackier than the painting, but tried to be diplomatic. "It's very . . . interesting. It reminds me of a trapeze at a circus."

"Don't say that too loudly. When these miners get a little high, they're as wild as coyotes. One of them might decide to take a little swing with Bertha and Charlie there."

"I'll be careful." Sierra grinned as she followed Melanie around a curve in the hallway, toward the stairs. The smell of beer and smoke hung so heavily in the air, the ornate ceiling fans served only to stir, not dispel it. The tinkling of the upright player piano across the room could barely be heard above the laughter and voices of the men at the tables. "Is there anything else I should know?" Sierra asked.

"Not really. On the whole we have a pretty good clientele." Melanie frowned as she nodded at a huge man in a red flannel shirt seated at a table near the bar. "Try to stay away from Sam Beattie. Let the bartender Monty Jackson wait on his table. Beattie's a troublemaker and poison-mean when he's drunk."

Sierra shivered. "He looks as if he could be. He reminds me of Brutus in those Popeye cartoons."

"Well, you won't find anything funny about Sam. The only reason we let him in here is that he usually causes more trouble when we try to keep him out." Melanie gave her arm a quick, comforting squeeze. "There's not many like him, and you won't have any problem with the girls or Monty. You'll like Monty."

In the next hour Sierra found she was right. She did like big, cheerful Monty and found most of the customers equally good-natured and helpful. Many were occupied with the various card games being offered at the tables, and those who weren't were just as involved with one of Melanie's luscious "doves." However, when any one of them became too involved, he was whisked upstairs by his "dove" or Melanie with speed and discretion.

Sierra was at the bar loading her tray for the umpteenth time and congratulating herself on her smooth entry into the scene when a familiar clipped voice spoke at her elbow. "You could have mentioned the precise nature of your intended occupation in your note."

"Deuce." She turned with a smile. It was good to see a familiar face among all these strangers. "Didn't I tell you that? I guess I was in such a hurry that I forgot. But you can see, I'm getting along fine, and there's really nothing to worry about."

"I'm sure you're hardly capable of judging how well you're 'getting along' after only an hour," Deuce said caustically. "Just because you haven't been involved in an outright orgy doesn't mean your situation around here couldn't become a bit dicey."

She shook her head. "No one's going to pay any attention to me with all those gorgeous girls in the same room. And everyone is being very polite."

"How jolly." Deuce's expression was remarkably lacking in enthusiasm. "However, I don't think you'll find York equally polite when he shows up here. I recommend you come home now and avoid the inevitable explosion."

She met his eyes. "But it's not home to me," she said softly. "I have no place there. You've both been very kind to me, but I can't stay anywhere that I can't pull my weight. York wouldn't listen to me, so I had to take matters into my own hands." She forced a tremulous smile. "I'm sure York will be glad that I'm out of his hair, once he finds out I'm perfectly all right. He admitted he wished I'd never come to Hell's Bluff."

"Did he indeed?" Deuce's lips tightened to a thin line. "Well, then he has no right to complain, has he?" He rested his left foot on the brass rail of the bar. "And I'll take great pleasure in sticking around to tell him so." He gestured to the bartender. "Give me a brandy, Monty. Carry on, Sierra. I think I'll just have a drink and keep you company for a bit."

She had no need of company for the next fifteen minutes as she flew from bar to tables and back again. She was too breathless to exchange more than a smile with Deuce, but it gave her a warm, comfortable feeling to know he was there. As much as she had denied having a home here, Deuce seemed like family.

She was loading her tray for another venture into the thickening crowd when Deuce's murmur in her ear caused her to nearly drop the glass she was holding. "Don't look now, but I believe the cavalry's arrived." His gaze was on the wooden swinging doors at the front of the saloon. "The *full* cavalry. You've never met the other two Delaneys, have you?"

"No." Her eyes widened in surprise as she twisted around to try to peer through the crowd. "What are they doing in Hell's Bluff?"

"Does there have to be a reason? The Delaney brothers are very close." A smile tugged at Deuce's lips. "Now why does this little scene remind me of the confrontation at the O.K. Corral? Doc Holliday and the Earp brothers?"

"They all had drooping mustaches," Sierra said absently, her attention on the three men standing in the doorway. The Delaney brothers might be clean-shaven, but an aura of power and danger surrounded them. Though they were dressed in the same rough attire of jeans, boots, and jackets as the rest of the men in the room, they possessed a presence that was totally different . . . and riveting. She swallowed. "They're very impressive, aren't they? Which is which?"

"Rafe is the gypsy-looking one on York's left," Deuce said. "Burke's the bloke who looks like he eats nails for breakfast."

"And does he?"

"No, he eats corporations for breakfast."

Sierra could believe it. Burke's craggy face held a hint of ruthlessness as well as strength. Her gaze slid to Rafe Delaney. Gypsy. Deuce certainly had a concise way with descriptions. Rafe's dark face was also strong, but held none of Burke's ruthlessness. His winged brows and bright eyes gave an impression of such vitality and joie de vivre, Sierra involuntarily found herself smiling at him. Just then his gaze encountered hers, and he smiled, too, with beguiling charm. He turned to York and said something.

Sierra forgot about the corporation devourer and the gypsy as York's gaze located and pinned her in place. A fire ignited in his eyes. Then he was striding across the room with such explosive determination that the crowd parted before him as the Red Sea did for Moses.

Sierra felt a tiny flicker of panic that she forcefully stilled at birth. She had expected this meeting, and there was nothing to be apprehensive about. She lifted her chin. "Hello, York. I'm sorry, but I can't talk to you right now. I'm very busy, as you can see." She picked up the tray, trying desperately to remember which table had ordered the drinks. "There's really nothing to say anyway if you read my note."

York took the tray and set it back on the bar. "You've just retired," he said flatly. "We're leaving. Go get your coat."

"I'm not leaving." Her voice was even, and her gaze steady. "I've been hired to be a waitress here, and that's what I intend to be. It's been pointed out to me that this is the one spot in town you don't own, so you have nothing to say about it. You wanted me out of your life and I'm out. Discussion closed."

"The hell it is." His eyes were blazing down at her. "I guarantee that you'll learn more than one thing a day here. The men who frequent the Dove will be happy to teach you all sorts of tricks." His gaze fell on Deuce, leaning indolently against the bar. "You look very comfortable. Why the devil haven't you gotten her out of here before this?"

Deuce shook his head. "I wouldn't think of it. I'm opting out, York." He smiled faintly. "From what Sierra tells me, you dug this particular trench yourself. I'm going to stand here and watch you dig your way out or wallow in the mire."

"Thanks a lot."

"Introduce us, York." It was the gypsy, Rafe, at York's shoulder. Burke Delaney was standing beside him. Both men nodded at Deuce, then looked pointedly again at Sierra.

"Sierra Smith, my brothers Rafe and Burke," York said without looking away from Sierra. His smile was suddenly warm and coaxing, lighting that wonderful face with special beauty. "Come home, Sierra," he said in a voice of velvet softness. "This is no place for you. We'll work something out.

She was almost lost for a moment. She shook her head to toss off the silken threads of charm he was weaving around her. He was doing it deliberately. She could sense the hard edge of anger beneath that velvet. "It's my job now," she said. "Until I move on, the Dove is my place." She picked up the tray again. "And I've already worked something out, haven't you noticed?" She ducked around the three men. "Excuse me, I have work to do."

"Not for long," York said grimly. "I'll just have a word with Melanie."

"I told her you would," Sierra said. "Feel free. I don't think she'll be impressed. She strikes me as a very independent lady." She disappeared into the crowd.

"She's right, you know," Deuce said. "Melanie doesn't like being told what to do."

"I know," York said between his teeth. "She's almost as stubborn as Sierra."

"What are we going to do now?" Rafe asked. His eyes were dancing. "I pictured you throwing her over your shoulder and striding out through those swinging doors. You're a big disappointment to me, York."

"It may come to that yet. We're sure as hell not leaving here without her. Find a table and get yourselves a drink. I'm going to hunt up Melanie and try to talk some sense into her." He scowled at Deuce. "Join us by all means, if you don't consider me too far beyond the pale to associate with."

"I'd be delighted. Sierra seems to be scoring off you quite splendidly. Do you think I'd miss a chance of watching the show at close quarters?"

"Perish the thought." York turned toward the stairs. "We mustn't deprive you of a single particle of amusement."

For the next hour Sierra caught only fleeting glimpses of Rafe and Burke Delaney, sitting at a table by the front door, as she hurried about the room. As the evening wore on, the milling crowd increased, and it became difficult to retain sight of anyone. She had no time to worry about them anyway. It was hard enough just to keep going when her breath was growing more shallow and her legs weaker with every trip through the throng.

"All right?" Monty asked as he set two beer mugs on her tray. "Why don't you take a break? I can hold things down here."

"A little later maybe." She smiled gratefully. "When the crowd thins out." A tiny frown wrinkled her brow. "It does thin out, doesn't it?"

"Not much."

"Rats." She picked up the tray. "We'll see." She moved briskly toward a table near the bar. She had almost reached it when she felt a tugging at her skirt. She glanced over her shoulder with a smile that died instantly. It was Brutus. No, she corrected herself, Sam Beattie, but close up he looked even more like the cartoon villain. A five o'clock shadow gave his face a sinister air, and his eyes . . . She moistened her lower lip nervously. "Did you need something?"

The other three men at the table laughed, and she felt the color rise to her face. Lord, what a stupid thing to say in a place like this. Beattie's cohorts were obviously as unpleasant as Beattie himself.

"Attention," Beattie answered. He leaned back insolently in his chair, still holding her skirt. "I don't like Monty waiting on our table. Why can't we have a little 'personal' service?" He showed his crooked teeth in an unpleasant smile. "Maybe I shouldn't complain. I overheard you turning the boss man down a while ago. I liked that. The Delaneys think they own the whole damn world."

"Personal" service. The double entendre was

clear, Sierra mused, but she tried to ignore it. "We're too busy for one person to handle everyone. Monty is only helping me. I'll be glad to tell him you need something."

Beattie shook his head. "Monty can't give me what I need." The short blond man on Beattie's right snickered. "I want to sample the boss's private stock."

She shifted her hold on the tray so she could release one hand. "Not possible." She jerked her skirt out of Beattie's grasp and stepped quickly out of range. "I'll send Monty." She turned and hurried to the table that had been her original goal. Her hands were shaking slightly as she set the beers down. She mustn't be so frightened. Beattie was undoubtedly unpleasant, even menacing, but nothing could happen to her in a crowd like this.

Yet that self-admonition did little to reassure her as she caught Beattie's narrowed gaze on her several times in the next ten minutes. Then, to her intense relief, she saw him rise unsteadily to his feet, weave across the room, and start up the staircase. Evidently he was going in search of more willing prey.

York passed Beattie as he came down the stairs, and by his expression Sierra could tell he had gotten nowhere with Melanie. She should have been pleased, but wasn't. The glance he threw at her as he strode past the bar was filled with frustration, exasperation, and something else. Pain? Oh, damn, she didn't *want* York to worry like this about her.

"Well, if you're not going to take a break," Monty said, "will you do me a favor? I need some clean bar towels. Will you run upstairs to the linen closet and get them for me?"

She pulled her attention from York's unyielding back. "Sure, Monty. How many?"

"Five or six will do." He nodded at a polished oak door at the far end of the bar. "Better take the service staircase to the second floor. We wouldn't want any of the boys to see you go and think you might get lonely up there. The linen closet is the first door to the left at the head of the stairs." He grinned. "Make sure you don't get the wrong door. Sometimes the customers get a little peeved when their privacy is invaded."

"I can imagine." Sierra cast a quick glance at the balcony landing. Beattie was nowhere in sight. He must be occupied behind one of those closed doors, she thought. At least she wouldn't have to worry about him for the rest of the evening. "I'll be right back," she said, and walked briskly toward the door Monty indicated.

"And just where the hell do you think you're going?"

York. How had he gotten across the room so quickly? She turned, her hand on the knob of the service door. "I'm running an errand for Monty. Not that it's any of your business."

"Have him send someone else," he said curtly. "I don't want you out of my sight for the short time you'll be here."

"It's part of my job. I can't tell him—" She broke off. "Oh, for goodness' sake, I'm just going to the linen closet. Will you please sit down and leave me *alone*?"

"No." He leaned one elbow on the bar. "I'm going to stand right here and not take my eyes off this door. If you're not back in ten minutes, I'm coming after you."

"York . . ." She could see by the grimness of his expression arguing would be futile. Her lips tightened with anoyance as she opened the door. "Oh, do what you like."

"That would be a novelty, at least. Ten minutes."

The heavy oak door closed behind her. The short hallway leading to the austere concrete steps of the service staircase was brightly lit, but she still felt isolated. No smoke, no noise, no Wild West decor. The silence was curiously jarring, even . . . threatening. She shook her head impatiently at the thought and swiftly climbed the steps. York's unreasonable concern must be clouding her judgment, she thought, for her to have this weird reaction to such commonplace surroundings.

She opened the door at the top of the steps. As she stepped onto the balcony landing, she was immediately aware again of the noise and smoke. The first door to the left, Monty had said. She opened the door and flicked on the light. Stacks of sheets, blankets, and towels of every size and description neatly lined the shelves. The closet itself was as large as a small room. It took her less than a minute to locate the bar towels. She picked up half a dozen from the shelf, flicked off the light, and closed the door behind her as she stepped back into the hall.

A large meaty hand closed on her arm. "Come on."

She glanced up swiftly. Beattie. Her heart jerked with shock and the beginning of fear. Heavens, he was a monster. Six feet five at least and as brawny as Paul Bunyan. She suddenly felt very small and ineffectual with that huge hand wrapped around her wrist. "I beg your pardon?"

"I said, come on." Beattie's voice was slurred and he was swaying slightly. Poison-mean when he was drunk, Melanie had said. As he continued there was no doubt about either his inebriation or his viciousness. "Nice of you to save me the trouble of coming down to get you. I've got a room for us just down the hall."

"No, you don't understand. That's not my job

and—" His hand tightened on her arm with bruising force, and she gasped with pain. The bar towels fell to the floor. "Let me go!"

"You wouldn't be here if it wasn't your job." His arm slid about her waist, and his fingers dug painfully into her side. "Everyone in town knows you've been shacking up with Delaney." He sneered. "Did you get bored and want a little variety? Well, I'm your man. I can show you ways of doing it that— Ouch!"

He didn't release her as she'd hoped, but the kick to his left shin had at least broken off that slimy proposition. "I told you to let me go," she whispered with fury. "Take your hands off me or I'll scream the house down."

"The hell you will." The expression on Beattie's face was ugly. "You'll come along and give me what I want. Ain't I good enough for you?" He started down the hall half carrying her. "I'm tired of being spit on."

"You can't do this." She was pulling desperately at the hand on her waist.

"I'm doing it." He glanced down at her with drunken malevolence. "If you so much as peep, I'll break your ribs." His hand tightened cruelly and she inhaled sharply. He could do it, she thought. That broad, powerful hand was granite-hard. That he would do it wasn't even in question. *Poison-mean.* The phrase ran through her mind as he swept her along in his wake. She could feel that poison flowing out of him, touching her with its acid. She cast a furtive glance at the barroom below. No one was even noticing them. The sight of a couple walking along this corridor was a common occurrence, and the veil of smoke and noise was a barrier almost impossible to overcome. She couldn't even see the table where the Delaneys were sitting. She turned her head and caught a glimpse of York standing at the bar. His gaze was fixed broodingly on the service door beside the bar just as he'd told her it would be. Look up, she commanded silently. For heaven's sake, look *up*, York.

What was she doing? she asked herself. Just because she was frightened, she wanted to run to York for protection. This situation wasn't any different from any other in her life. She was capable of handling it just as she had the others. Think. She had to think. Fear was tightening the muscles of her stomach and making her feel slightly sick. He was so *big*. If he got her into one of those rooms, she'd be as helpless as a child.

"That's my little girl," he said as he reached for the knob on a door. "I won't hurt you as long as you let me—"

His arm at her waist had loosened a trifle. She wouldn't have another chance. She jabbed him in the ribs with her elbow at the same time she whirled away, breaking free of that clamp on her side. He was solid as a stone wall, but at least she had broken his hold. She backed away from him, her breath coming in little gasps.

"Bitch!" He was lumbering after her, as menacing as a wounded grizzly bear. "That was a mistake. You're not going to like what I'm going to do to you now."

She kept backing down the hall. Which room was Melanie's office? Sierra asked herself. It was on the other side of the landing. She'd never make it before he caught her. She couldn't make it to the stairs either. He was blocking the hall.

He smiled nastily. "Scared? You should be."

She searched wildly for a way out. Then she saw it. *Bertha and Charlie!* She kicked off her high heels and ran down the hall. She heard a low curse, then Beattie's pounding footsteps behind her. She climbed over the rail of the balcony and edged out on the six-inch ledge to cling desperately to the support post.

"What the hell!" Beattie was right behind her, reaching out for her. She couldn't wait any longer. She released the post and leaped. Her hands touched the bar of the dove swing and she held on. She'd made it! The silver cords seemed to give a little with her slight weight, and the plaster of Paris doves swayed drunkenly on their perch.

She heard a sudden outcry from below as someone caught sight of her hanging from the swing. Then there was laughing and applauding—even a few whistles. Oh, Lord, they thought it was some kind of a prank. Except for York. She could see him looking up at her in stunned disbelief, mouthing words she couldn't hear.

"York," she called desperately. She swung back as far as she could until she was against the ornate post that supported the second floor balcony. "Catch me!"

She pushed away from the post, swinging her lower body to gain momentum. Her palms burned with the friction of the strain she was placing on them. Once, twice, three times. She could see a blur of movement below her. York? It was now or never.

She closed her eyes as she released the bar. If he wasn't able to catch her, she certainly didn't want to know about it ahead of time. She fell swiftly through the smoke-filled air.

Strong arms snatched her out of that air and cradled her in a protective embrace. Enormous relief surged through her, making her dizzy. "York," she whispered.

"Burke."

Her eyes flew open and she found herself looking into green eyes, not blue. The brother who ate corporations for breakfast.

"I was closest," he explained with the faintest flicker of humor. He inclined his head politely. "How do you do?"

"Much better than a few minutes ago."

"I should imagine." He turned as York ran up to him. "Your property, I believe." He transferred her into York's arms. "You should fatten her up though. She doesn't weigh more than a feather."

York's arms tightened around her possessively. "No, she doesn't," he said hoarsely. He was oddly pale, and a muscle was jerking in his cheek. He seemed to be having trouble getting the words out. "Thanks, Burke. I don't think I could have gotten here in time."

Burke nodded. "Anytime. My pleasure. May I suggest that you get her out of here? By the look of that man charging down the stairs, she won't be safe for long."

"The devil she won't." Rafe Delaney was suddenly beside them, his face as hard as his voice was soft. A reckless lopsided grin curved his lips. "What do you say we eliminate her problem?"

"No," Sierra said quickly. "I don't want any trouble. He has friends . . ." Those friends were already pushing their chairs away from the table, she noticed frantically. "Let me down. This is my problem, not yours."

Beattie skidded to a stop before them. His eyes were filled with malice. "Give her to me."

"No."

She had become a bone to be fought over by two bulldogs, she thought half hysterically. It would have been funny if the air hadn't been charged with such menace.

Beattie took a step closer, reaching for her.

"Deuce." York's voice cut sharply through the suddenly quiet room. "Take her. And, for Pete's sake, watch out for her."

She was being thrust into another pair of arms. Deuce's this time. This was crazy. She felt like a product on an assembly line. She heard Beattie's violent curse as Deuce turned away. "Stop," she said. "Let me down, Deuce. I have to—" The room exploded behind her, and she strained her head back to see what was happening.

Fists were flying, chairs breaking, curses being shouted. She caught a glimpse of York's savagely joyful smile as he closed in on Beattie. "No," she whispered. She was suddenly struggling wildly in Deuce's arms. "Why are you doing this? York will be hurt. I have to get to him."

"York said to take care of you," Deuce said. Then, as she continued to struggle, he added testily, "Will you stop that? I'm no Hercules like the Delaneys, you know. How can I be expected to manfully whisk you out of here if you won't cooperate?"

"Do you think I'll leave here when they're *killing* each other back there?"

"Obviously not." He sighed. "All right, we'll stay." He set her on her feet, then dropped to his knees, jerking her down with him. "We'll compromise. Come on." He crawled beneath a table, pulling her after him. "I discovered a long time ago the best place to be in a barroom brawl is under something. You can see what's going on, and hopefully no one can see you."

"But I don't want—"

"Here or outside." Deuce's voice was clipped and utterly decisive. "You'll only distract York and possibly get him hurt running around out there. Which is it?"

"Here," Sierra said with a sigh. "But I can't see very well." There was a discordant tinkle as someone or something was thrown against the player piano. "There were only Beattie and his three friends against the Delaneys. Now everyone in the room is fighting. How did that happen?"

"It would take hours to explain the philosophy of the domino effect as illustrated by a barroom brawl," Deuce said lightly. "I considered writing a book about it once, but—"

"Beattie's down!" Sierra clutched Deuce's arm excitedly. "I see his face lying on the floor beside that pair of black boots."

"Only his face?" Deuce murmured. "Interesting. York must have been a tad more upset than I thought."

"You know what I mean. I don't see York. Shouldn't the fight be over now?"

"Sorry, Sierra. It doesn't work that way. You'll know it's over when it gets very quiet." A table laden with beer glasses crashed to the floor and splintered. "Not yet, obviously."

"People are being hurt out there." She bit her lip. "York or his brothers could be—"

Deuce shook his head. "I've seen the Delaney brothers brawl before. I assure you, they give considerably more punishment than they receive."

"There's always a first time. What if—" She stopped. The chaos had abruptly subsided, and there was only one low thread of sound. Someone was laughing!

Deuce smiled faintly. "Rafe. Come on, I guess it's over." He took her arm and helped her from beneath the table.

York, Burke, and Rafe were standing by the bar and, as far as Sierra could tell, they were the only ones left standing. The room looked as though it were the product of a nightmare: broken glass, overturned tables, chairs, men lying unconscious on the floor or sitting up looking around dazedly. She heard a man groan and looked up to see the blond man who'd been at Beattie's table sprawled on the stairs. Melanie's girls were clustered on the second floor balcony looking down at the wreckage in stunned disbelief.

Melanie herself was descending the staircase like a vengeful Valkyrie. "York, what the hell do you mean doing a job on my place? You come in here busting—"

York raised his hand. "What the insurance doesn't cover, I'll pay. It was worth it. You'd better send for the doctor. I think he has a little minor patching up to do."

"The three of you look like you could do with a little patching yourselves," Melanie said as her gaze drifted from battered face to battered face.

"We'll tend to it at home." York turned and caught sight of Sierra. His smiled faded. "And we *are* going home, Sierra. I don't think Melanie is going to risk this happening again."

Melanie shook her head regretfully. "It was a mistake. I knew a house had to be one way or the other. I'm sorry, Sierra."

"I'm the one who's sorry," Sierra said huskily. "I didn't mean for any of this to happen. If there's anything I can do to help clean up. . . ."

"You just run along," Melanie said. "We'll take care of it." She sounded the faintest bit nervous. "I'll even have one of the girls pack up your clothes and have them sent to you. There's absolutely no need for you to stick around."

"All right." Sierra turned to York. "I'll come with you, but nothing is really settled, you know. We have the same problem."

"We'll talk about it later." York started for the door. "At the moment the only thing I'm interested in is going home and getting in the shower to steam some of the sting out of these bruises." He grinned back over his shoulder at Burke and Rafe.

"There are only two bathrooms at the house. Do we draw straws to see who has to wait?"

Rafe looked shocked. "Really, York, you know Mother always told you that guests go first. I'm surprised at you."

"And the eldest always takes precedence," Burke drawled. "The two of you can fight it out for the other bathroom."

York shook his head. "Why do I have a feeling that I'm going to come in last again?"

"You didn't come in last in the fight tonight," Burke said gravely. "Every time I see you as strong and as tough as Old Nick, I want to shout or pray or . . ." His voice trailed off. "Oh, what the hell. Let's get to those showers." He strode past York and pushed out the swinging doors.

York and Rafe followed more slowly, and Sierra could hear Rafe's low laugh as he clapped York affectionately on the shoulder. She turned to Deuce. "What was that all about?"

He shrugged. "York will probably tell you about it later. There's nothing to be upset about. He and his brothers are very close, but they don't mean to shut other people out. It just happens."

Sierra looked after them wistfully. "I'm not upset. A little envious perhaps. That must be a wonderful feeling."

Deuce nodded. "You're not alone. I'm sometimes out in the cold too." He smiled. "Now shall we toddle on home and bandage the wounded gladiators?"

She grinned back at him and fell into step as he strolled toward the swinging oak door.

Sierra placed the piece of raw steak carefully on Rafe's eye. "I've always wondered if this really did any good," she said. "Wouldn't an ice bag do just as well?"

Rafe grinned. "Probably. However, traditions must be observed. We Delaneys are great ones for traditions."

Sierra glanced across the kitchen table where Deuce was carefully applying antiseptic to the shallow cut over Burke's right eye. "You seem to have fared a great deal worse than Burke. All he has is the bruise on his cheekbone and that cut."

"I fight harder," Rafe said complacently. "I'm surprised Burke wasn't under that table with you and Deuce."

Burke made a sound that fell somewhere between a growl and a snort. "You mean, you're more reckless. How many times have I told you that fighting is a science?"

"This eye isn't too bad," Sierra said. "but your nose is going to look like an elephant's trunk for a day or so, Rafe." She frowned. "Do you think it's broken?"

"More than likely. It's been broken twice before, so it's prone to fractures." He flinched as she carefully put a bandage over the bridge of his nose. "I don't think it's too bad. The last time it hurt a hell of a lot more than this." He glanced at Burke. "Did you notice that all York got was a cut lip?" He grinned. "I told him he must have done some fancy dancing to protect that classy profile."

"I'm surprised you didn't get the other eye blackened," Burke said. "York appeared to be a bit uptight before he went upstairs to shower."

Rafe nodded. "I think he restrained himself because my bruised and battered condition was earned in his cause."

"But it wasn't his cause," Sierra said. "It was mine. I can't tell you how terrible I feel that you were even involved, much less hurt, because of me." Her eyes filled with tears. "I'm so very sorry."

Rafe smiled gently. "Don't worry about it. These things happen." His dark gypsy eyes were suddenly twinkling. "According to York and Burke, they happen to me more often than to either of them, but don't you believe it."

"Believe it," Burke said. He looked seriously at Sierra. "And don't have any regrets on my account. I needed what happened tonight. I've been under a hell of a strain lately, and that explosion provided me with a much needed release."

"Some release." Sierra's smile was a little shaky. "You both could have been seriously hurt."

"But we weren't," Rafe said cheerfully. "And it was a damn good brawl."

Deuce stepped back from Burke and capped the antiseptic. "That's as good as I can do. Do you want a Band-Aid over it?"

Burke shook his head. "It will be better to let the air get to it."

"Right." Deuce glanced at Sierra inquiringly. "Did you take care of that cut of York's before you went upstairs?"

"No." She lowered her eyes. "Will you do it, Deuce? I think I'll go to bed. I'm very tired."

"Sure." Deuce nodded with understanding. "Why don't you run along right now? One brawl is enough for tonight."

She smiled sadly. "There won't be a brawl. We just have to come to an understanding, and I don't want to involve Rafe and Burke any further in my problems." She turned back to the Delaneys. "Will I see you in the morning?"

Rafe shook his head. "I have to get back and so does Burke. We'll be leaving at sunrise."

"Then I'll say good-bye as well as good-night now.

I'm sorry I didn't get a chance to know both of you under more serene circumstances."

"Another time," Rafe said. "I'll look forward to it."

She made a face. "I doubt that's true after all the trouble I've caused you, but it's kind of you to say it."

Burke smiled. "Well, you have to admit that a situation like this has a tendency to strip off all the superficialities of a relationship."

She nodded. "Yes, it does. Thank you again for catching me. Even Papa Marino couldn't have made a better catch."

"You're very welcome." Burke lifted a brow. "I assume this Marino is one of your old vaudeville friends York told us about."

"Acrobats." She became very still. "York must have gone into my past history very thoroughly with you. This wasn't just a casual family visit, was it? York sent for you because of me." She held up her hand when she saw both hesitate. "You don't have to answer that. I don't mean to make the situation any more awkward for you than it is already." Her cheeks were flushed as she turned away. "I'm just sorry York thought it necessary to—" she gestured helplessly with one hand. "I'm just sorry, darn it." She almost ran from the room toward the stairs, half blinded by tears.

"Sierra."

York was standing on the landing of the stairs. His hair was still damp from the shower, and his eyes were dark with concern. "What's wrong?"

"So much trouble," she whispered brokenly. "You shouldn't have done it, York. I told you I couldn't stand being a charity case. You shouldn't have . . ." She pushed past him and leaped up the stairs.

He stared after her, half tempted to follow her. He

was experiencing again that agonizingly poignant pain of empathy. They were both on edge right now, and it would be better to let a little time pass before they tried to talk. Heaven knew, his own emotions were in tatters tonight, and if he followed her to her room, he would probably end up doing exactly what he'd been trying to avoid.

He looked up at Rising Star's serene countenance. "Were you this much trouble to Joshua?" he murmured. "It's no wonder the poor guy never married again." He stood there a minute longer before turning and descending the rest of the stairs.

Deuce had broken out the brandy in truly generous and clearly unmedicinal quantities and handed York his glass as soon as he came into the kitchen. "Mind that lip," he warned. "This alcohol will sting like the devil."

It did sting, but it was worth it. York downed the brandy and held out his glass. "More."

Deuce obliged. "I'm obviously not going to have to put antiseptic on your wound as Sierra asked me to do. If you continue imbibing like that, your cut will not only be clean, it will be sterile. I'm not saying what it'll do to your head, however."

"It can't be any more messed up than it is right now." He looked at Burke and Rafe over the rim of his glass. "Don't worry, I'm not going to pressure you to take Sierra. After tonight I realize I couldn't let her out of my sight, even with one of you playing guardian. I'd be going crazy wondering what the hell she was getting herself into."

Burke and Rafe exchanged glances.

"We thought you'd come to that conclusion," Burke said. "Your expression when you saw Sierra hanging from that swing was very . . . revealing."

York suppressed a shudder. He didn't like to think of that moment. He took another sip of his brandy. "I don't doubt it. I felt as if someone had reached in and pulled out my guts."

Deuce looked a trifle pained. "That sounds exceedingly gory."

"But accurate," York said. "Exceedingly accurate." He lifted his glass in a slight toast to Rafe and Burke. "Thanks for coming; I'm only sorry it was for nothing. I'll have to work out my own problem."

"We'll always come when you need us, York," Rafe said quietly. "And we'll always be here for you." He paused. "I only hope you'll still be here for us to come to."

York smiled self-mockingly. "You've been getting vibrations? I've been trying to work my way through it."

"If we can help, let us know." Burke finished his drink and stood up. "Now I think I'll hit the sack. At least this is one night I won't have trouble sleeping."

Rafe's curiosity had been intensely piqued. "Are you having trouble—" He stopped. "Never mind. Even if you'd tell me, I'm not sure I'd want to know at the moment. There'll be time for that later, when I've recovered from the memory of that big-eyed nymph flying through the air." He leaned back in his chair and held out his glass to Deuce for a refill. "Though, in retrospect, it was amusing to see your waif and those weird-looking plaster doves sharing the same perch."

"It will have to be considerably further in the future for me to appreciate the humor of the situation," York said. "You're not going to bed?"

Rafe shook his head. "I'm too restless." His gaze was innocent as he said kindly, "But you and Burke run along. We young bucks don't need as much sleep as you old geezers. Maybe I can talk Deuce into a game of poker."

"Delighted," Deuce drawled. "I can always count on you to have a sense of humor regarding my little idiosyncrasy. York has been most unreasonable about it of late."

"If you make it an all-night affair, brew a pot of coffee for us in the morning," York said. "I'll be up at five to drive you to the heliport."

"I'll drive them," Deuce offered. "You sleep late and rest your battered bones."

York shook his head. "I'll do it. I can sleep anytime, and I don't see these characters nearly often enough to suit me." He grimaced. "Besides, it won't be a chore getting up at dawn. I've been restless as hell myself lately." He caught Rafe's suddenly alert glance and shook his head warningly. "Come on, Burke. Like the kid said, it's time we old geezers got to bed."

Seven

Sierra didn't awaken until late afternoon the next day. It didn't particularly surprise her since she hadn't gone to sleep until after dawn. She had still been lying in bed wide-awake when she had heard York's and his brothers' footsteps in the hall, Rafe's low infectious laugh, the slam of the front door, and the roar of the Jeep in the early-morning stillness.

There had also been a stillness within her by that time. After a night of thinking she had finally come to a realization, an acceptance, and then a decision. That decision had brought peace, and after that, she had dropped off to sleep with no problem. She woke with the same inner tranquillity and contentment, and after she had showered and dressed in her usual casual attire of T-shirt and jeans, she ventured downstairs to find York.

Deuce was sitting at the kitchen table drinking coffee, and glanced up when she walked into the room. "Well, you certainty don't appear to be tottering on the brink of nervous prostration," he said dryly. "In fact, you look to be in a hell of a lot better shape than I am."

"I feel fine," she said as she crossed the room. She opened a cabinet and took down a cup and saucer. "I wish I could say the same for you. Those circles of dissipation under your eyes would do credit to the portrait of Dorian Gray. You look worse than the Delaneys did after the brawl."

"I was up all night with that limb of Satan, Rafe," Deuce growled. "He not only drank me under the table, he had the audacity to take advantage of my inebriation to manipulate the cards to his own advantage." He took a sip of coffee. "I was most indignant."

"He *cheated* you?"

Deuce was immediately on the defensive. "If I'd been myself, he would never have been able to do it, you understand. I haven't been duped like that since I was twelve years old."

Sierra was having trouble keeping a straight face and turned quickly to pour her coffee. That wicked gypsy devil, she thought. "I'm sure you were grossly misused." She disguised a gurgle of laughter with a cough. "Where's York?"

"Down at the mine. He stuck around here until afternoon waiting for Sleeping Beauty to awaken. He even took a peek in your room a few times to make sure you hadn't had a heart seizure and died in your sleep."

"Did he?" She felt a warm stirring at his concern. She took a sip of coffee and lowered her gaze to the cup she was cradling in her hands. "I'm sorry he was worried. I had some thinking to do and didn't get to sleep right away."

"That's what York finally decided." Deuce paused. "He thought you'd still be upset when you woke up. That's why he left me here on guard. He wasn't sure which way you'd fly." He squinted speculatively at her. "But you aren't upset, are you?"

"No, I'm not upset any longer." She glanced up and smiled. "And I don't intend to fly anywhere at the moment, so you can join York at the office if you like, though I'd recommend you swallow a few aspirins and take a nap instead." Her expression became totally deadpan. "Your experience with Rafe was obviously very traumatic."

"It was, indeed, but I learned a solid lesson from it."

"Not to cheat?"

"Certainly not," he said, outraged. "A man doesn't give up his art because of one trifling misjudgment. No, I've just resolved never to cross bottles with Rafe Delaney again." He set his coffee cup down and stood. "And I think I'll follow your advice and pamper my bruised ego as well as this ghastly hangover with a short nap. York won't need me; he'll be tied up until late this evening. He has to go straight from the office to the Soiled Dove. Melanie's insurance man is flying in to discuss compensation for last night's rhubarb." He lifted a brow. "You're sure I can trust you not to run away again?"

"You can trust me. I'm through running. It's time I faced the situation head-on and came to terms with it."

He gave a low whistle. "That sounds like York may be up against more than he's bargained for." He hesitated. "Don't be too rough on him, Sierra. He's only doing what he thinks is best for you. York's problem is that when he becomes involved with people, he usually cares too much."

She knew that. York cared for Deuce and his brothers with a single-minded devotion she was beginning to envy. The bond of caring had been evident with his every word and gesture when he was with them. She felt a twinge of pain as she realized that York might never give her the same affection. Oh, well, she would take what she could get. She had learned a long time ago that dreams seldom come true for people like her. "I'm sure you're right, Deuce," she said gently. "He cares very much for you, I know."

He nodded. "I'm one of the select few. York doesn't let many people close to him. Rafe and Burke were born into the magic circle, and I blundered in through circumstances and blind luck."

"Blind luck?"

"A little play on words." His smile was bitter. "I couldn't resist it. York happened on the scene at the precise moment a nasty bloke deprived me of my left eye with a stiletto. He was trying to do the same to the right eye when York stopped him. Very violently and efficiently."

"Good God!" Sierra stared at him in horror.

"I must admit at that moment I doubted the goodness of God and for that matter the entire universe." He touched his black eye patch. "I'm not a man who is grateful for small mercies. I wanted both eyes." He shook his head. "I was a complete son of a bitch for a number of months. Not many people would have put up with me. But York did. He got me to a doctor, then stayed with me through all the raving and the cursing." His voice dropped to a mere whisper. "And the weeping. Hell, and we weren't even friends before that night in the bar."

Sierra's throat was so tight, she could scarcely swallow. "And you've been together ever since?"

He nodded. "He won't admit it, but I think the only reason he came back to the States was because he wanted to make sure I didn't lose the other eye in a similar situation." He smiled faintly.

"Here in Hell's Bluff York feels he can control the situation better. York is a man who instinctively takes charge. It's a facet of his character." His voice became coaxing. "Let him take charge for a little while, Sierra. You won't regret it. I never have."

"Don't worry. I'm not going to cause York any other difficulties. I think I've found a solution that will take care of everything." She made a face. "However, it may take a little adjusting on his part."

"Adjusting?" Deuce asked warily. "York's not accustomed to adjusting."

"Too bad." She turned to the sink and began to rinse her cup.

"Sierra, I don't—" Deuce stopped. She could feel his gaze on her back, but she didn't look around. When he spoke again, his tone was resigned. "You'd think by now I'd have learned not to interfere. I much prefer a spectator's role. I'll call York and tell him you're neither suicidal nor swooning with grief. I'll leave him to discover on his own what else he has in store."

She heard Deuce's retreating footsteps as he left the room. Her hands were trembling a little as she set her cup in the drainer to dry. That first euphoric serenity was beginning to crumble. The fluttering in her stomach was increasing by the minute, and she mustn't let that happen. She must take everything minute by minute and not think ahead. She must certainly not think of York or tonight.

She was gone!

Her bed was neatly made and her bedroom dark and deserted. York flicked on the light switch, fully expecting to see a note on the bedside table or her pillow. She hadn't been downstairs in the parlor when he had come home, nor in the kitchen, the library . . . Where the hell was she?

He should never have gone to the Dove tonight, he thought. These negotiations with the insurance people had stretched on for hours. If he'd had any sense, he would have realized Sierra would do something impulsive. She'd obviously been desperately unhappy last night.

Yet Deuce had said she hadn't appeared overly upset this afternoon. Deuce's reassurance had been the only reason he had been able to make himself stay and go through all that maddening red tape at Melanie's.

No note. However, the absence of a note didn't necessarily mean she hadn't run away. She could be out there alone and— Waves of panic surged over him as he spun and bolted out of the room. Where the hell was Deuce? This silence was far too much like last night when he had come home to find Sierra gone. There hadn't been a note from Deuce downstairs, so he, at least, must still be in the house.

York pounded loudly and impatiently on Deuce's bedroom door with his fist. "Deuce, open the door. Where the hell is she? You said—"

"Deuce isn't home."

Sierra's voice! Relief caused the blood to drain suddenly from his head, making him weak. "Where have you been?" he asked as he turned around. "I've been looking all over the—" He stopped. Sierra was standing in the open doorway of *his* room. "Is there something wrong? Are you waiting for me?"

"Yes, I am waiting for you." She slowly backed into the room, her dark and solemn gaze fixed on him with trepidation. "Come in."

"Thank you," he said ironically as he strolled down the hall toward her. "That's very kind of you.

Why couldn't you have waited downstairs to talk to me? Though I don't know why I expected that. You never do what anyone else would do."

"I thought it would be more convenient here." Oh, dear, she thought. This was even more difficult than she had expected. "I didn't mean to impose, but I—"

"For heaven's sake, you're not imposing," he said irritably. "I didn't mean to imply that, and I didn't mean to be sarcastic either. You just scared the hell out of me and I was striking back." He stopped a few feet from where she was standing in the middle of his room. "Now why don't we go downstairs and make some coffee and talk? We have to come to an understanding. I don't think either of us wants a repeat of what happened yesterday." He smiled crookedly. "I'm not sure either of us would survive it."

"I'm not sure, either," she whispered. "I couldn't go through that again. Oh, not what happened at the Dove. That was bad enough, but when I realized all the trouble I'd been . . ." She shook her head. "It has to end, York. We're at an impasse. You won't let me go, and I can't stay without giving." She walked slowly toward him. Her face was pale and her eyes desperately earnest. "Shut the door."

He stared at her. "What?"

She shut the door herself and turned the lock. "We have to end it." She faced him. "Make love to me, York."

He went still. The room was suddenly charged with tension. He swore softly and fluently. "This is crazy. In case you haven't noticed, I've been trying to avoid that very thing like the plague for some time," he said harshly. "I've told you how idiotic it would be for us to become involved sexually. I've told you that you're too— What are you doing?"

"Getting undressed." She was unbuttoning her tailored shirt. Her hands were trembling so much, it was taking an eternity. She was nervous enough without worrying about buttons. "I was thinking about already being undressed when you got here, but I didn't know what your reaction would be."

"The same as it is right now. Rejection."

She shook her head. "That wouldn't have bothered me. I've dealt with rejection before. Most of the time you just have to grit your teeth and plow straight ahead." She had the blasted buttons unfastened at last, and she slipped out of the shirt with a sigh of relief. "It's just that I'm not experienced at all this, and I was afraid I'd appear more funny than seductive." She didn't look at him as she undid the front closing of her bra. "The perfect compromise would have been a marvelously flimsy nightgown, but I didn't have anything but my old faded pajamas. They definitely would have struck you as funny." She shrugged out of her bra as casually as possible and dropped it on the chair by the door.

"I don't think so," he said. "I'm sure as hell not laughing now."

She looked up swiftly. He was staring at her naked breasts. The intensity of his gaze made her catch her breath and the muscles of her stomach tighten. "Good," she said shakily. "Because I couldn't be more serious about this." She kicked off her shoes and began to unfasten her jeans. "I could handle it if you did think it was amusing, but it's much—"

"*Stop*, dammit." York's voice was low and vibrated with tension. "This is . . . You don't want to do this."

"How do you know I don't? Have you ever asked me?" She slid the jeans down and stepped out of them. "All you've ever done is tell me how vulnerable I am and how terrible you'd be for me." Her hands went to her bikini panties. "You never gave me a choice."

"For heaven's sake, will you put your clothes back on?" His hands were clenched into fists at his sides. She could see desire burning in his eyes. . . .

"No, I'm seducing you." She tried to keep her voice steady. "I've made up my mind, so you might just as well resign yourself." She drew a shaky breath and smiled up at him. "However, I'd really appreciate it if you'd show me how to go about it."

"*Why?* Why are you doing this, Sierra?" He seemed to be having trouble speaking. His gaze had fallen from her breasts to her hands, which were hesitating on the band of her panties.

Because I love you. The words were so close, they were trembling on her lips. *Because I can't let pass the opportunity to belong to you, even if it's only for a few weeks, or a few hours.* She knew she couldn't say those words. She couldn't say anything that would reveal her vulnerability to him. As it was, he already felt far too responsible for her. She couldn't saddle him with the knowledge of a love he might not be able to return.

"Because this is the solution," she said instead. "You want me. You told me so yourself, and it's making you uncomfortable and unhappy because you think you can't have me." She shook her head. "It's the same problem Deuce told me your men experience here in Hell's Bluff. Lack of availability. Well, I'm making myself available."

"And paying off what you conceive as your debt at the same time." Anger was mixed with the desire in his eyes now. "We've gone a long way past the proposition I made you during those first days after I brought you here. You can't earn your keep that way, Sierra."

"Can't I?" She smiled at him lovingly as she took a step toward him. "Why don't you let me try?"

"The hell I will. If you want to prostitute yourself, go back to Melanie's."

"I can't. You and your brothers closed the place down." She moved closer. "Why are you so angry? I'm only trying to give you what you want."

"I don't want . . ." He paused to steady his voice. "Put on your clothes, Sierra. Please."

She shook her head. Her hands reached up and began to unbutton his shirt. "I've made up my mind. It took me a long time to do it, but I'm not about to change it now."

"Stop that." He caught her wrists. Her skin was warm and soft. Her arms were so slender, his fingers could easily encircle them. He wanted to run his hands up her arms to her fine-boned shoulders, then tilt back her head so her throat was open and available to him as it had been that night in the parlor. The muscles in his stomach were knotting, and the aching tension in his loins was blurring everything but its mindless urgency. Nothing seemed more important than satisfying that hunger. Yet he knew there were more important things to consider. There was Sierra and what was best for her. "Step aside," he said. "If you won't leave, I will."

"I'll just follow you." Her voice was firm. "We're alone in the house. I asked Deuce to go to the dining hall for the evening. You can't get away from me by stalking out of here." She had finished unbuttoning his shirt and now pulled it open. The well-developed muscles of his chest were as beautiful as the rest of him. A wedge of dark springy hair dusted that chest, and a beaten silver and turquoise necklace gave him a slightly barbaric air. "I'll follow you wherever you go." She slid her arms around his waist and nestled against him. The feel of his warm skin and the abrasion of hair against her nipples was like a hot tingling shock. She gasped as a shiver ran through her. "Hadn't you better give up?"

"Sierra." His hands hovered over her naked shoulders. Her hair smelled clean and faintly floral, and he could feel her hard nipples pressing against his flesh. White-hot waves of sensation were rolling over him. "Please . . ." His throat was dry and raspy, and the words wouldn't come. "Stop plowing ahead. I can't *take* anymore."

"That's the point of being persistent." Her lips moved across his chest, and her teeth pulled teasingly at a tuft of hair. "To batter down resistance." She suddenly closed her eyes and sagged against him. "Don't make me do this alone any longer, York. It's very difficult for me."

"Is it?" Aching tenderness filled him at her confession, banishing resistance as desire had not. She was so small and delicate—despite her strength of will. He touched her shoulders tentatively. "You're sure this is what you want? I can't talk you out of it?"

"I'm sure."

His hands slid down her naked back, his fingers exploring the hollow of her spine. Protectiveness and a passionate possessiveness flooded him. "Then you're not alone any longer. We're in this together."

She snuggled closer. "Well, that's a relief. I'm certain you're much better at seduction than I am."

He felt his throat tighten and his hands were gentle as he pushed her away. "I doubt that very much. I've never felt more seduced in my life. What a bold vamp you've turned out to be, Sierra Smith." His gaze was running over her, and the tenderness shifted to tension once again. "And what a lovely one."

Color rushed to her cheeks. "I didn't think I'd feel this shy. Sleeping in the same room with two parents and four siblings isn't calculated to inspire any great degree of modesty." She touched the bikini panties. "Shall I get rid of these now?"

"Leave them on. You look very provocative." He stripped off his shirt and threw it on a chair. "There's plenty of time to do that later. Seduction should be slow and easy."

"Should it?" she murmured. The light from the single lamp gleamed on his sun-bronzed skin and caught the silver of his necklace. His beautiful eyes had darkened and she wanted to stand there and look at him forever.

She was gazing at him with the same breathless joy she had that night in the moonlight, he thought, and suddenly felt within him the exuberant happiness he saw in her face. It was so strong, he had to wait for a moment before he was able to answer her.

"I'm not sure," he said, "that a slow and easy seduction will be possible tonight. Go over and sit on the bed, love. I want you out of reach while I finish undressing."

He watched her cross the room to the big four poster bed. She was tiny, yet every curve was perfectly formed. Her white skin looked like velvet and her dark hair gleamed in the soft light. Instead of sitting on the bed, she knelt, her gaze eagerly fixed on him. "Hurry," she said. "Get undressed. I want to look at you. You're so—" She broke off as he frowned at her. Then she grinned unrepentantly. "I'm sorry. But you are, you know."

He was undoing his belt and his lips curved in a smile of resignation. "A peacock? What the hell am I going to do with you?" He held up his hand as she opened her mouth to answer. "Never mind, I have a few ideas on that score myself." His voice lowered

threw back his head and arched his spine as if he were being tortured. "Love me, York."

He looked down at her with an expression of unbearable torment. "Sierra, it's getting out of control. I can't hold on. I don't want to hurt you."

"You won't hurt me." He was the one in pain. She could feel the agony of tension gripping every muscle in his body. Why wouldn't he give in to it? Then, incredibly, he was moving away, leaving her! "No!" Her hands grabbed his hips, her legs winding about him, holding him to her. "No, York, don't do this. . . ."

"Sierra." His chest was heaving as though his lungs were starved for oxygen. "You don't know. I'll hurt you again."

"My choice." Her voice was fierce as she began to move slowly, seductively against him. "Not yours. *Now*, York."

"Sierra!" His control shattered and he plunged forward, shocking, stretching, filling. Then the fiery rhythm began, and Sierra became lost and yet found. How could that be? she wondered hazily. Impossible? No, nothing was impossible while this miracle of sensation existed. It existed for a long time, spiraling from one brilliance to another.

She could sense even in the midst of the storm York was trying to be careful, but she wouldn't allow it. She was wildly delighted to discover a touch of her hand, a teasingly seductive movement of her hips, could make him forget everything but the primitive pleasure she was giving him.

Then she herself forgot about seduction as tension began to mount within her to dizzying heights. Her head thrashed back and forth on the pillow, and she had to bite her lip to keep from moaning. "York . . ."

"I know." His voice was harsh with passion. He was lifting her into each thrust, striving for greater closeness, more depth, a merging so complete, it was unbelievable. Slick and hot and hard. "Soon, love."

It was no longer soon but now. Here. Rapture and closeness. A joining that gave joy and ecstasy and, at last, peace.

York's body was heavy as it lay on hers, trembling in the aftermath of that storm of emotion. She was trembling, too, and she couldn't seem to come to terms with the fact that it was really over. How could something so powerful have subsided in one glorious burst of sensation? Then she felt a stirring within her and knew it wasn't over. "York?"

He raised up, resting his weight on his arms on either side of her. His eyes were still smoky with need and slightly bewildered. "It's never happened to me before." He laughed a little. "I want you again and I haven't even left you."

She smiled up at him. "What's the problem? We'll make love again. I'm just getting the hang of it anyway."

Something flickered in his face and his lips curved in a gentle smile. "Oh, no. You've done enough seducing for one night. I think it's time I took charge for a change. You're too generous for your own good."

A lock of dark hair had tumbled over his forehead and she felt a sudden urge to brush that lock away with loving possessiveness. Why not? Perhaps for a little while she could even pretend he belonged to her. "Deuce said you're a man who takes charge."

"When I'm allowed," he said dryly. "With the two of you that's not always possible. This time, however, I'm going to insist. I can wait now." He flexed slowly. "I hope." He bent swiftly and kissed her.

"But I'll stay here for a few minutes, if it's okay with you. You feel so damn good."

"I don't mind." She loved it. In some ways it was even better than the wild joining that had gone before. She felt part of him.

He pulled away slightly. "You're so little. Are you sure I'm not hurting you?" His hand caressed her belly.

"You're not hurting me. I like it." Lord, she loved him. She loved his gentleness and his caring and the way he was looking at her as if she were very special. It was like being sheltered beneath the red velvet canopy of her childhood dream. As long as he held her like this the dream existed.

He was smiling faintly as he looked down at her. "Hey, come back to me. What are you thinking about?"

She sighed contentedly. "A canopy bed. I was thinking you remind me of one."

His smile widened to a grin. "Well, that's different anyway. You mean I've finally wooed you away from the notion that I'm a peacock? Praise be and hallelujah!"

"At the moment. Why can't you be both?"

"I imagine you'll give me no choice." He kissed her again, long and lovingly. "I'm leaving you now. Thank you for your hospitality, love." He shifted off her and she instantly felt vulnerable and alone again.

He pulled the sheet over them and drew her back into his arms. She nestled close, her cheek against the warm hardness of his chest. "Anytime," she said. For the rest of her life, she thought: anytime, anywhere, anyplace.

"I wish you wouldn't say that. I'm having a rough enough time trying to be patient." His lips drifted over the delicate skin at her temple. His voice abruptly lost its lightness. "This isn't a panacea, you know. We're going to have to discuss this takeover move on your part."

"I didn't think it would be a panacea, but it did help," she said as she tightened her arm around his waist. "You're happier now and so am I." She lifted her head to look at him with sudden uncertainty. "You are happier, aren't you?"

He was silent for a moment, then pushed her head back on his shoulder. "I'm happier," he said gruffly. "I don't have any idea how I'm going to feel when I'm able to think again, but I'm happy as hell right now."

"Then we'll work the rest out later."

She rubbed her cheek lovingly against him. She didn't want to think of later. Right now he belonged to her. It couldn't last, Sierra told herself, but this present was worth any price she might have to pay in the future. Something rough scratched against her cheek. The silver necklace. She reached up to touch it, running her fingers over the smooth turquoise. It was warm from his body heat and felt almost alive.

"I like this," she said softly. "It looks strong and durable, yet the workmanship is exquisite. It surprised me when I saw you wearing it." She chuckled. "Considering your aversion to peacock comparisons, I thought you'd hate jewelery."

"I do. I've just worn the necklace so long, I'd feel uncomfortable without it. My mother put it on me one night when I was about six. I was in the hospital and I guess she thought it would make me feel better. It belonged to Rising Star and was supposedly blessed by the shaman of her tribe. I guess my mother would have tried almost anything to help me at that point. She knew I was terrified. I'd just found out I was going to die."

Sierra's head lifted swiftly. "What?"

"I'd been ill all my life. People were always telling

me I mustn't run like Rafe and Burke. I mustn't get too tired. I mustn't ride anything but the gentlest of horses." His mouth twisted in a bitter smile. "My life was full of mustn'ts. I never understood why until I entered the hospital when I was six for tests and found out I had a heart ailment that was going to kill me before I reached my teens."

Her eyes widened with horror. "They *told* you that?"

He shook his head. "I overheard the nurses talking outside my room. My mother was furious, but she didn't lie to me when I asked her. She knew I would find out eventually. She just told me she and my dad were doing everything possible and I must help too. The next night she brought the necklace to the hospital and gave it to me."

How terrible it must have been for both mother and son, Sierra thought. The little boy frightened and helpless in the face of something he couldn't possibly understand. The mother also frightened and unable to offer her son even the protection of ignorance.

"Well, it must have worked," Sierra said. She tried to keep her voice steady. "You're obviously healthy as a horse now. Did the medical world make one of their breakthroughs about that time?"

"No. I just grew out of it. When I went back to the hospital when I was twelve for tests, they found that I was perfectly normal." He shook his head. "They called it one of those freak recoveries, a miracle cure."

A miracle, she thought. If that miracle hadn't happened, York wouldn't be here now. She would never have met him, never have loved him. It was impossible to imagine a world without York. Strange and terrifying. She shivered and instinctively dropped her head back on his chest so she could hear the throb of his heart. It was reassuringly strong and steady, and she felt a surge of relief. He was well now. How idiotic to be frightened of an ailment that had corrected itself over twenty years ago.

"Your parents must have been ecstatic after worrying all those years," she said, "and you must have felt you'd been given the world on a platter."

His hand tangled in her sleek hair. "I don't think I really believed it at first. It was hard to realize there was a future out there for me. When I accepted the fact it truly was in the cards, I went a little wild." His chuckle held a note of dryness. "Hell, I went crazy-wild. I think my parents had it easier when all they had to worry about was me keeling over from heart failure. I just couldn't settle down to being a part of Killara like Burke and Rafe."

"That was probably a natural reaction. They couldn't expect you to go through something like that without being scarred." She didn't know how he had survived at all. What a nightmare of a childhood he must have had with that nemesis constantly in the background. "I bet they didn't mind one bit."

"Well, let's just say they were very understanding. So were Burke and Rafe, for that matter. I was damn lucky to have them."

And *she* was damn lucky to have him. Sierra was swept by a wave of love and thanksgiving so strong, she couldn't speak for a moment. He was *alive.* Her throat was achingly tight as she lifted her head to look at him. "I'm glad you decided to stick around until I came along." She carefully kept her tone light. "You know how important learning something new every day is to me. You've contributed enormously to my education tonight."

He gently cupped her face in his hands. His

expression was very grave. "Not nearly as much as you have to mine, Sierra. I hope you don't regret it." The gravity vanished as a teasing grin touched his lips. "But I believe you told me you promised yourself you would learn at least *one* new thing." He suddenly rolled her over. "You'd be surprised at how accomplished a tutor I can be. Why should we stop at just one?"

His dark head was lowering slowly toward her and she could sense the tension charging his body. She began to feel the same languid breathlessness she'd known such a short time before. Her arms slid lovingly over his shoulders and around his neck. "No reason in the world," she murmured.

Eight

The early-morning sunlight polished York's dark hair to a deep sheen and revealed the stark perfection of his profile against the pillow. Beautiful, Sierra thought. If she lived to be a hundred and fifty she'd never see a sight more beautiful than York lying relaxed and asleep after a night of love.

And it had been love, she told herself. Not only on her part but on his as well. There had been too much tenderness, too much emotion behind every caress, every word, to have been mere lust. Yet never once during the night had he admitted to feeling more than desire. She had known seducing him would be a gamble, but she had thought it would be worth it. Now, as she stood looking down at York with a love stronger than anything she had ever imagined, she wasn't so sure. Passion had only honed her love, giving it a two-edged sharpness. Even if York did love her, it didn't mean he'd immediately confess it and ask her to stay with him. He was a complicated man, and there were aspects of his personality that were a mystery to her.

She let out a long breath, hoping to release the tension that had been building within her. The dice had been thrown, and all she could do was wait until York awoke to see if her gamble had come up seven or snake eyes. She turned and walked swiftly to the door.

She closed it behind her carefully, and started down the stairs. She didn't want to be in bed beside York when he woke. In that first moment there would be no barriers, and what if she saw only regret? It would be better to wait and erect a few barriers herself before she had to face that possibility.

Rising Star's eyes seemed to hold both compassion and understanding as Sierra paused on the landing to look up at her. "Well, I did it," she whispered. "These Delaney men aren't easy, are they? Wish me luck." No answer. What had she expected anyway? Still, she did feel a little more tranquil as she continued down the stairs to the kitchen.

Deuce was standing by the counter reaching for the coffeepot. He looked up as she came into the room. "Coffee?" he asked.

"Please." She got down two cups and saucers from the cabinet and set them on the counter. "You look much better than you did yesterday. Hangover all gone?"

"It wasn't the hangover, it was the blow to my self-esteem that laid me low." Deuce poured the coffee into the cups. "However, a night at the gambling table with a few of the miners soon put me right. I had a very successful evening." He looked up at her. "And how successful was your night?"

She felt the color rise to her cheeks. She had

known when she'd asked Deuce to leave last night that he'd had his suspicions. "I don't know. We'll have to see."

"This isn't what I meant when I told you to let York take charge, you know." Deuce grimaced. "It was a very dangerous gamble, Sierra."

She lowered her gaze to her cup. "He cares about me. I know he does."

"York won't accept any love that threatens to tie him down," Deuce said. His voice was warm with sympathy. "He loves Killara and his brothers, too, but even they may not be able to hold him. There's a good chance you may be backing a losing horse."

"I hope not." She lifted her cup to her lips, still not meeting his eyes. Every word Deuce had said had pricked her like tiny sharp needles. "I had to try, Deuce. I didn't have any choice."

He sighed. "Sometimes we don't, love."

"Is there enough coffee in that pot for me?" York suddenly asked. He stood in the doorway.

Shock jolted through Sierra's body. He must have awakened immediately after she had left the bedroom. She turned to see him standing in the doorway. He wasn't looking at her at all, but at Deuce. She experienced a strong sinking sensation that made her feel sick. Snake eyes. The dice had turned up snake eyes.

"Plenty," Deuce said. "Get another cup and saucer, Sierra."

"I'll get it." York strode across the room, still avoiding Sierra's gaze. She found herself avoiding his as well. She didn't want to see the pain and awkwardness she knew must be there. As he filled his cup he was only inches away from her. She could feel the heat from his body and see the tension that was gripping him. "How's it going, Deuce?" he asked.

"Very sticky, I would say," Deuce said dryly. He

set his cup and saucer down on the counter. "I believe I suddenly remember duties elsewhere. I'll see you both later."

"No, Deuce, it's—" Sierra stopped. It was no use trying to keep Deuce as a bulwark against the confrontation to come. It would only be a cowardly postponement.

Deuce paused at the door to meet her gaze. "A very dangerous gamble, Sierra," he said. His glance suddenly flicked to York. "Oh, I almost forgot to tell you. Rafe called this morning."

"Does he want me to call him back?"

"No, he just told me to give you a message. He said he'd thought about your problem and worked out a solution. He was sending it by helicopter." He glanced at his watch. "At ten this morning. That's about thirty minutes from now. Do you want me to drive down and pick it up?"

York shook his head. "I'll do it myself. You'd better go down to the office and see if there's anything important I should attend to."

"Right."

York turned to face Sierra as soon as he heard the front door close behind Deuce. "We have to talk."

"Why?" She couldn't keep the bitterness from her voice. "I'm not obtuse. I know what you want to say."

"Do you?" He met her gaze at last and she was startled by the torment she saw there. "I don't want to say it. Can't you see that? All I want to do is pick you up and carry you back upstairs. I want to lock the door and keep you in bed for the next week."

"But that's not what you're going to do, is it?" she asked dully. "You're going to tell me I have to go away."

"I can't do that either. I'd go crazy wondering what was happening to you." He shook his head wearily. "I don't know. Maybe I'm the one who should go away. I could leave Deuce here to watch over you."

"No!" She set her cup down almost angrily. "This is your home. I won't run you out of it. I'll be the one—"

"Dammit, Sierra, don't you realize the situation has changed now? How can I let you leave after last night?" His eyes darkened. "I went crazy. I didn't think of anything but loving you. I didn't *protect* you. You could be carrying my child."

Her eyes widened in surprise. "I could, couldn't I?" she whispered. She hadn't thought of that. She felt a surge of heady joy rise within her. She might not be able to have York, but there was a possibility she could have this child. "I've always wanted a baby."

"Sierra . . ." York's eyes were suddenly glowing with tenderness. "What am I going to do with you? Don't you know that's not the reaction a woman is supposed to have at the possibility of an illegitimate child?"

"Isn't it?" She smiled shakily. "But that's how I feel. Don't worry, York. No responsibility, no paternity suit, no ties. Last night was all my doing, and if there's a child, that will be mine, too."

"The hell it will." His mouth tightened grimly. "If you remember, I participated very actively in the procedure. It will be my baby. What kind of irresponsible idiot do you think I am?" He ran his hand distractedly through his hair. "What am I saying? There may not even be a baby, but it's a possibility we have to take into consideration. There's one thing for sure, I'm not going to be able to stay around here until we know one way or the other." He slowly reached out and touched her neck. She shivered and swayed toward him. "I'm aching. I want to take off your clothes and sit down

Now why don't you go upstairs and rest? I'll bring your suitcase right up."

Kathleen shook her head so hard, the coronet of braids quivered. "I'm not the least bit tired. As soon as I change my clothes, I'll come down and start cooking you a nice roast for lunch."

York's eyes widened in alarm. "No need for that. I wouldn't think of imposing on you, Kath. I'll just keep having the meals sent up from the dining hall. It's enough that you came when I needed you."

"Nonsense. Acting as a chaperon is no job at all. I might as well keep myself busy while I'm here. Maybe I'll make a tapioca pudding too. You've always liked my puddings."

York was turning a little pale. "Yes, I always did." He cast Sierra a desperate glance. "But Sierra can't stand pudding, can you, Sierra?"

"What?" He was glaring at her with such menace, she was having difficulty keeping a straight face. "Oh, no, I can't say I really care for them."

Kathleen nodded. "No puddings. I'll just have to make one for Mr. York some other time. I'll make gingerbread instead. Do you like gingerbread, Miss Sierra?"

"Just Sierra," she corrected Kathleen. "And I like gingerbread very much."

Kathleen gazed at her for a thoughtful moment. "No, I think it's definitely *Miss* Sierra." She smiled mysteriously. "It's truly going to be a fine spring, isn't it?" She didn't wait for an answer but bustled into the house, humming softly beneath her breath.

After the door had closed behind her Sierra turned to York. "How's the gingerbread?"

"Almost as bad as the tapioca. You should have blacklisted it along with the pudding."

She shook her head. "It wouldn't have been plausible. Gingerbread is so . . . homey. Besides, I couldn't imagine anyone making gingerbread inedible."

"You'll see. I'll call Deuce and tell him to stop by the dispensary and bring home some antacid pills."

"She can't be that bad a cook," Sierra said. "I like her."

"And I love her." He smiled. "When we were kids, it was always Kathleen who played games and covered for us when we were in trouble. We're all crazy about Kathleen." Then he made a face. "But I swear the Spanish Inquisition could have used her. One bite of her gingerbread and a victim would have confessed anything to avoid another one."

Sierra laughed. "I gather we're all on a diet."

He started to nod, then stopped. "Not you. You need good square meals. I'll have Deuce smuggle you in something."

"That won't be necessary. I won't be here that long. Kathleen's arrival doesn't really change anything, York."

"Oh, yes, it does." His voice was determined. "I'm not at all sure Rafe's intentions were benevolent, but for once his prank is going to pay dividends. As a chaperon, Kathleen is totally formidable. There's no question I'll be allowed within a mile of your bed while she's on the premises. If you'll agree to remain here until we know whether or not there's going to be a child, I'll stay too. Please, Sierra, it means a hell of a lot to me."

He was so dear, she thought as emotion tightened her throat. She didn't want to leave him. Perhaps, if she gave it a little more time, there might still be hope of him accepting what they could have together. "All right," she said. "I'll stay."

His breath released in a little burst of relief. He

reached out to caress the soft hair at her temple. "Thank you. I'll try to stay out of your way as much as possible."

When she tried to smile, she found her lips were trembling. "Are you sure you're not just trying to avoid Kathleen's cooking?"

His fingertips followed one pointed strand to her cheekbone. "Oh, yes, I'm very sure." His eyes were suspiciously bright. "Seeing you would be much more dangerous than Kath's worst effort. A bellyache doesn't have a patch on a heartache. Take it from one who knows." His hand fell away from her cheek. "I'd better get out of here. I'm beginning to feel my willpower sliding into a bottomless pit. I'm going down to the office. Tell Kath I'll be back for supper."

She followed him to the edge of the porch. He glanced back at her as he went down the stairs. "Don't look at me like that." His voice was rough with feeling. "Can't you see I'm doing what's best for you? Isn't it better I leave you now than later?"

She didn't answer. She couldn't answer. She could only look at him and love him and try to still the hurt.

His own eyes were dark with pain. Then, with a muttered curse, he tore his gaze away and strode around the house to the Jeep.

Nine

Four nights later a shrill sound broke the stillness inside the house. It was so piercing it startled Sierra from the depths of sleep. She sat bolt upright and fumbled for the switch on the lamp beside her bed. The terrifying noise was cut off abruptly, then she heard voices in the corridor.

She jumped out of bed, grabbed her robe, and threw open the bedroom door. York was already barreling down the stairs, his shirttail out and his hair still mussed from sleep.

Deuce garbed only in a wine-colored brocade robe, was standing in the doorway of his room. "Where's the trouble, York?" he asked.

"Shamrock," York called over his shoulder. "Call the heliport and tell them to have the copter ready for me when I get there."

"Right."

Kathleen joined Deuce in the hall as the front door slammed behind York. Her red hair was tumbling wildly about her shoulders. "Mr. Rafe?" She clutched the collar of her flowered cotton duster nervously. "What kind of trouble?"

"We don't know yet. York will call us as soon as he gets to the ranch." Deuce was halfway down the stairs on his way to the study.

Sierra shook her head dazedly. "What's happening?"

"The alarm went off." Kathleen licked her lips nervously. "It means trouble."

"What alarm?"

"The Delaney properties are linked by a special security system. When there's a problem at the ranch, Delaney Tower, Killara, or Hell's Bluff an alarm goes off automatically at the other places."

"Perhaps it's a false alarm," Sierra said. Kathleen was so frightened, she was beginning to be frightened herself. "I've heard that happens sometimes."

Kathleen shook her head. "No, the alarm goes off first at the trouble spot. There's a five-minute grace period for it to be canceled before the alarm rings at the other places. Mr. Rafe didn't cancel it, and that means it's no false alarm. He needs help. There's some danger at Shamrock."

Danger. There was danger, and York was walking right into it. Icy fear clawed at her. She had a sudden desire to rush after him and make him take her with him. She wanted to shelter him from that danger. She knew she couldn't do that. It was too late. He would probably be boarding the helicopter any minute now. Deuce was right. York would surely call as soon as possible. Oh, Lord, she hoped he would remember to call.

She turned to Kathleen and gave her a quick hug. "Go back to bed. It's still the middle of the night. York and Burke won't let anything happen to Rafe. They look out for each other, remember?"

Kathleen shook her head. "I couldn't sleep now."

Sierra knew she wouldn't be able to sleep either. "Then let's go down to the study with Deuce and wait. I don't think any of us are going to get any more rest until we get that call."

The phone call didn't come until just after sunrise. Deuce leaped for the receiver with an alacrity that belied his usual sangfroid. He listened for a moment, then murmured a quiet good-bye. He turned immediately to Kathleen and Sierra who were tensely waiting. "It's okay. It was a fire. Quite a bad one evidently, but no injuries. York will be back later this morning and let us know the details."

"Thank the Lord," Kathleen murmured.

Sierra wanted to echo the words. She felt limp with relief. "He's all right?"

"Everyone is all right," Deuce said gently. "Now I suggest the three of us adjourn to our separate chambers and get some sleep."

Sierra stood up. "Yes." She doubted if she'd sleep, but she couldn't stay here. She felt too raw and vulnerable. The hours of fear and tension had stripped her of all protective barriers. Only the love and pain were left. She walked swiftly toward the door, wanting only to escape. "Good night. I mean, good morning." She almost ran from the room.

Kathleen looked up with a bright smile as Sierra entered the library. "You slept late this morning," she said. "That's real good, Miss Sierra. I was afraid you'd be too upset to rest properly after all that hullabaloo. I haven't liked those circles beneath your eyes one bit."

"I guess I've been bothered by insomnia. It's probably a reaction to all those vitamin pills I've been taking."

Sierra dropped into the brass-studded leather easy chair and watched idly as Kathleen whisked about the room with a feather duster. It was really amazing, Sierra thought. She always felt as if she were watching a segment of *Ripley's Believe It or Not!* when she observed Kathleen clean house. No matter how assiduously Kathleen appeared to apply herself, the dirt remained untouched when she had finished. The phenomenon reminded Sierra of the character Pig Pen in the Charlie Brown cartoon.

"I'd probably sleep a good deal better," she said, "if you'd let me help around the house."

Kathleen shook her head. "It wouldn't be proper. Besides, you need all your strength. You hardly eat more than a bite or two at meals. It's a good thing I came when I did or you'd have gone straight downhill."

Sierra glanced hurriedly away. "Yes, you came just in the nick of time. But I never eat much even when I'm well. Has York come back from Shamrock?"

"No." Kathleen ran the duster over the mantel clock. "But I'm sure he'll be back any time now." She wrinkled her nose. "Providing the three of them don't get to palavering. They're all so busy running their own share of the business, sometimes they get a little carried away when they do manage to get to see each other."

The three musketeers," Sierra said flippantly. She doubted if York would be in any great hurry to get back. Since Kathleen had arrived, he had tried to avoid her at every turn. There were times when she had even been grateful for his absence. The sexual and emotional tension when they were together was almost as unbearable as not seeing him at all.

"Yes, thank the good Lord," Kathleen said softly.

"They were always close as boys, but it was different then. Now Mr. York can walk beside his brothers instead of trailing along behind."

"I can't imagine York trailing behind anyone."

"Neither could he. That was why it was so difficult for everyone. He loved Killara and the family with everything that was in him, and he wanted to belong in the same way Mr. Rafe and Mr. Burke did. It took him a long time to come to terms with his illness and realize he couldn't keep up with them."

"His childhood must have been a horror." Sierra shivered. "Children don't really understand death, but he still must have felt the stress surrounding him."

Kathleen shook her head. "Mr. York understood death. No one could have understood it better. He lived with it at his elbow every day. You could see him try to forget it and push it away, but something was always there to remind him." She pointed the feather duster at the clock on the mantel. "Did you notice how quiet this clock is? No gong to strike the hour, and the ticking is so soft, it would take a stethoscope to hear it. Every clock in the house is like that. Ever since he was a lad, he's hated the sound of a ticking clock." Her blue eyes were no longer bright but far away. "There's a clock at Killara that's a family heirloom; old Shamus brought it with him from Ireland. The ticking of that clock could be heard clear out in the hall. Mr. York couldn't stand that clock. He never said anything to anyone, but sometimes I'd see him standing there looking at it with his hands clenched at his sides as if every tick were a blow striking at him. It nearly broke my heart."

It would have broken her heart as well, Sierra knew. Just to picture the beautiful vulnerable child who had been York, standing there tortured and tormented by a fate he had no ability to change was enough to cause the tears to brim in her eyes. "I think I would have smashed the damn thing into a million pieces if I'd been he."

Kathleen turned away and began busily dusting the desk. "Strange that you say that. Someone did knock the clock off the mantel. It broke and never did work right after that happened."

"York?"

"None of the boys would confess who did it, so their mother punished all three of them." Kathleen looked up. "But not at all harshly. She was a very wise woman, that Mrs. Delaney."

Hot lemon juice and Rising Star's turquoise necklace, Sierra thought. "I only wish I could have known her. She must have been very special."

"That she was," Kathleen said softly. "I was only fifteen when I first came to Killara from Ireland. I was frightened and clumsy and so lonely, I would howl like a banshee in my bed at night. My sister, Bridget, was always the clever one, and I knew I could never measure up to her. Yet Mrs. Delaney never made me feel she thought less of me than she did of Bridget. I found a home with them, and her sons were my sons."

"A place," Sierra murmured. "You found your place in life."

"Yes, I found my place." Kathleen nodded vigorously. "I know I'll never be Bridget, but maybe I have qualities she'll never have either."

"I'm sure you have." Sierra walked across the room to Kathleen. "I think you may be a very special person too." She brushed her lips across Kathleen's plump cheek. "And I'm happy you've found your place. You're very lucky."

"I know that." Kathleen cleared her throat, then added gruffly, "Now that I'm finished in here, I'll get your breakfast. Come along to the kitchen."

Oh, dear. "I'm not very hungry, Kathleen." Sierra tried desperately to think of an excuse. "I thought I'd wait for lunch."

"Three meals a day." Kathleen took her by the arm and propelled her briskly toward the door. "No skipping breakfast for you, Miss Sierra. How do you expect to get well so that Mr. York can—" She stopped abruptly. "You need your strength."

Yes, she did, Sierra thought. It had become increasingly apparent to her that her stay at Hell's Bluff must end soon. She was going to need every bit of strength she could command, but she wasn't going to find it in one of Kathleen's ghastly gastronomical efforts. Yet how could she chance hurting the other woman? She sighed. "All right. I'll have breakfast."

Kathleen's beaming smile was almost worth the concession. Sierra tucked her arm in Kathleen's as they left the library. "But let me make the coffee," Sierra said. Maybe if she brewed it strong enough, it would numb her taste buds. "You do entirely too much around here as it is. Let me hel—" She broke off as Kathleen gasped with surprise. She followed the housekeeper's astonished gaze and saw York.

"I was hoping I could sneak in and get upstairs before you saw me," he said. He closed the front door behind him. "I tried to clean up a little over at Rafe's place, but I'm still not exactly presentable."

That was a gross understatement. His jeans were smoke-blackened and grass-stained, and the left sleeve of his khaki shirt had been torn away to accommodate a white bandage wrapped around his upper arm.

"Glory be." Kathleen shook her head in wonder. "You look like you've been fighting a grizzly. What's wrong with your arm?"

"Nothing much." York didn't meet her eyes. "I

hurt it a little. Rafe's vet cleaned it up and slapped a bandage on me."

Kathleen snorted. "A fine thing. What does a veterinarian know about treating burns? I'm surprised he didn't rub you with horse liniment. You just go into the kitchen and sit down. I have some salve upstairs in my first-aid kit that will fix you up right as rain." She started up the stairs. "Miss Sierra, you get him a shot of brandy while I go fetch my tube of salve."

"Kathleen . . ." York hesitated. He finally released his breath in a tiny explosion of sound. "The salve won't do any good. It's not a burn."

Sierra's brow wrinkled in a frown. "But the fire? You said. . . ."

"There was a fire, a damn bad one." York's lips tightened. "But for a while the fire was the least of our worries." He gestured to the bandage. "This is a gunshot wound."

"Gunshot?" Sierra's eyes widened in horror. "You were *shot*?"

He nodded, his smile slightly lopsided. "I managed to get in the way of a bullet during a sniper attack. Rafe and Burke came out of it without a scratch."

"Thank the Lord," Kathleen said with heartfelt relief. "What happened? Did they catch him?"

York shook his head. "Not yet. He got away clean."

"A sniper," Sierra repeated dazedly. "Someone just tried to murder you. How can you be so calm about it?"

"I'm not calm; I'm mad as hell. But this isn't the first time the Delaneys have been under attack. It goes with the territory. We control a good-sized empire, and it's impossible to deal with thousands of people and their livelihoods without stepping on a few toes along the way. We've grown accustomed to taking a bit of flak. That's why we employ a security force."

"You're accustomed to *bullets*? That sniper could have killed you."

"He didn't. I told you, I just got in the way. It was pretty clear Burke was the target this time."

"This time." Next time it could be York. The thought made Sierra shiver with panic. What if he was wrong? What if the killer came after him again and—

"You should see a doctor," Kathleen said. "A gunshot wound is nothing to sneeze at."

"It's only a graze. A doctor would have to file a report, and the media would love to get hold of a juicy item like this and blow it out of all proportion. We'll take care of it ourselves. Burke's going to tell Cougar to increase security at every base of operation."

"Cougar?" Sierra asked.

"Cougar Jones is in charge of all Delaney security." York smiled faintly. "He's quite extraordinary. You'll find out that he's a very interesting man."

"Well, if you won't have the doctor, I'm still going to take a look at the wound." Kathleen started up the stairs again. "It's not fitting for a Delaney to be treated by a veterinarian. There's no telling what concoction the man put on you."

York opened his mouth to protest, then closed it again. It never did any good to argue when Kathleen's maternal instincts were aroused. He watched her until she reached the top of the stairs and disappeared down the hall. "I think she equates veterinarians with witch doctors," he said. "Do you suppose I'm—" He broke off. "Good Lord, you're white as a sheet. What's wrong?"

"Nothing. What could possibly be wrong?" Her voice was on the edge of splintering. She lifted a trembling hand to her throat. It was tight. She couldn't swallow. "You almost got yourself killed. It would be stupid to get upset about . . ." The tears were trickling helplessly down her cheeks. "Why should I . . ."

"Sierra." York's voice was aching with tenderness. "Don't. Please. You're breaking my heart."

"Am I?" She wished she were convinced she had the capability of breaking York Delaney's heart. In the past few days her conviction that he loved her had weakened drastically. "You mustn't pay any attention to me. It's this damn waif's face of mine. It'll get you every time."

He crossed the few feet separating them. "I have to pay attention to you." His hand feathered her cheek in the gentlest of caresses. "I don't seem to be able to pay attention to anything else these days."

"Me too." She nestled her cheek into his palm. He smelled of smoke and horse and sweat, but she didn't care. She wished she could stand there forever and let his scent and warmth and vitality surround her with its force. It seemed a thousand years since he had touched her with this loving tenderness. "Please don't get hurt again." She closed her eyes. "I couldn't stand it, York."

He was silent for a moment, and when he spoke his voice was unsteady. "Don't care so much, Sierra. I'm not worth it."

"I can't help it." Her lashes lifted to reveal eyes jewel-bright with tears. "I don't know any other way. I do care." Her voice suddenly vibrated with intensity. "I *care*, York, and I'll be damned if I'll be ashamed of it." She inhaled a quivering breath and took a step back. "It's a pretty wonderful gift I'm giving you and you're a fool to turn me down. I could make you so happy." She turned and began to climb the steps. "But not if you're stupid enough to get yourself killed. Take care of yourself, blast it." She passed Kathleen coming down the stairs. "I think you're wrong, Kathleen. It's entirely fitting for someone with the brains of a bird and the stubbornness of a mule to be treated by a vet."

Kathleen gave her a glance of shocked reproof. "Really, Miss Sierra, the boy is—"

"An idiot," Sierra finished. A few seconds later the door of her bedroom slammed shut behind her.

"Here's a letter for you," Deuce said to Sierra as he strolled into the parlor. "It arrived at the mine office in the first mail this morning, so I thought I'd bring it right up." He handed her a gaudy red, white, and blue envelope. "I wasn't sure whether to deliver it or salute it."

Sierra smiled as she took the letter. "It has to be from Chester Brady. He told me once that everyone should write letters on patriotic stationery. According to him, it has a psychological effect on the recipients and tends to influence them in your favor. He always used this particular stationery on bill collectors."

"It sounds like him." Deuce watched her open the envelope and scan the letter quickly. "Do I gather he's trying to influence you as well?"

She nodded. "He says they need me. He's enclosed a list of their stops for the next four weeks."

Deuce grimaced. "Something tells me I shouldn't have delivered that letter. York is going to be most displeased with me."

"Is he?" It had been over a week since York had returned from Rafe's horse ranch, and the situation between her and him was growing worse with every passing day. She hadn't seen him over a half dozen times, and those had been fraught with such pain, it was becoming intolerable. "Perhaps you're mistaken. I just don't know anymore."

"Well, I do. York will go wild if he finds out you're planning on going back to Brady's glorified slave labor camp." Deuce paused. "And you're thinking of doing just that, aren't you?"

"It's very tempting. Chester said the magic phrase. He needs me. Heaven knows, no one around here does." She looked up at Deuce. "Do me a favor and don't tell York I received this letter."

He slowly shook his head. "I can't do that, Sierra. I'm not known for my loyalty, but what there is belongs to York. When the chips are down that's the way it has to be. I will make a bargain with you though. Why don't you think about this? York's leaving in about thirty minutes for a board meeting in Tucson. If you'll promise not to take off while he's gone and give him a chance to persuade you to his way of thinking, I'll hold off a bit on telling him about Chester's bid. Deal?"

She was tempted not to agree. It would have been so much easier to leave while York was away. However, the determination in Deuce's expression convinced her she had little choice. If she didn't agree, he would inform York about the letter at once, and she didn't think she could stand the explosion bound to follow. She needed time to marshal both strength and willpower. "Deal."

"Fine." Deuce smiled, and for an instant she saw a glimmer of affection in his face. "You won't be sorry. Second thoughts are nearly impossible to accept, but we have to do it at times."

She became very still. There was something important in what he had just said. The words were striking a note deep in her memory, like a bell ringing faintly in the distance. What was it?

She couldn't quite grasp what that beckoning memory was trying to tell her. Oh, well, it was probably nothing; she was so desperate, her imagination was probably playing tricks. "I suppose you're right," she said, "but I wouldn't count on the delay being of any benefit in this case."

He gazed at her in surprise. "But I always count on whatever I wish to happen. One only has to manipulate events as one does a deck of cards, with the most exquisite deftness and an occasional bit of sleight of hand."

She shook her head. "More than occasional, I would imagine. Is York leaving for the heliport from the office?"

"No, he's upstairs changing. Burke prefers the family to present a businesslike image at the board meetings. Since they take place only four times a year, York usually goes along with him." He studied her for a moment, his expression troubled. "I think I'll run along to the kitchen and ask Kathleen for a cup of coffee. Why don't you catch York before he leaves and tell him good-bye?" He didn't wait for a reply, but quickly left the parlor.

Lord, she thought, Deuce must be feeling self-sacrificing to brave Kathleen's coffee in order to give her the privacy he thought she needed with York. She wasn't even sure she wanted to see York before he left. What good would it do? Still, when she heard his footsteps on the stairs, she hurried out into the hall.

She had never seen York dressed in anything but jeans and a casual shirt. His black business suit was faultlessly tailored and formed an elegant contrast to his crisp white shirt and discreetly patterned gray tie. She felt as if she were confronting a stranger.

The look he gave her as he reached the bottom of the stairs was also a stranger's—guarded and remote and wary. "Hello," he said. "I thought you were in the kitchen with Kathleen."

"No." There didn't seem anything else to say. She felt awkward and tongue-tied. How could she love this stranger? Yet she did, and she could feel the pain begin to shimmer in waves around her. "I'm right here." What a stupid thing to say. She moistened her lips. "I mean, I thought I'd say good-bye. Deuce said you were going into Tucson. Are you spending the night?"

"Maybe. I don't know. The meeting usually lasts only a few hours, but I may decide to stay at the penthouse for a day or two. I need a change of scene." He met her eyes. "I told you I was like that."

"*Warned* is the word." Her voice was brittle. "Yes, I remember your warning. I remember everything you've ever said to me." Every touch, every variation of tone and expression, Sierra thought. She knew now she'd be tormented by those memories for the rest of her life.

There was a glint of pain in York's eyes before he quickly looked away. "I have to leave. I told them to have the helicopter revved up and waiting for me. I'll see you when I get back." He nodded jerkily and strode toward the front door.

"York."

He glanced back over his shoulder.

"Be careful. I've noticed whenever the three Delaneys get together, there appear to be fireworks."

"Don't worry. There's been no sign of that crazy sniper since the fire at Shamrock. Good-bye, Sierra."

He was leaving her. He was walking out of the front door and *leaving* her. Suddenly the intimidation and uncertainty binding her was blown away by a frustration that had been simmering far too long. She exploded with a fury that sent the blood pounding wildly through her veins.

She ran out the front door. York was already on

the red brick path leading to the driveway. "You stop right there," she yelled. Her hands were clenched into fists at her sides and her voice was shaking. "Do you hear me? Don't you *dare* walk away from me. This is all crazy. I can't stand it any longer."

He halted and turned to face her. "Sierra . . ."

"Don't you Sierra me." Her eyes were blazing in her white face. "What's so damn difficult about all this? I love you and I think you love me too."

"Sierra, that's not the question." His voice was infinitely weary. "It's whether I—"

"Don't pussyfoot around. Say it, dammit. *Say* you love me."

Suddenly his eyes were blazing too. "All right, I love you." He strode back up the walk and took the porch steps two at a time. "I love you so much I can't eat or sleep. I love you so much, it's tearing my guts out." His hands were on her shoulders, jerking her to him with a roughness that was close to desperation. "Dear Lord, *yes*, I love you." His kiss bruised her lips and made her head whirl. Then he was releasing her and running back down the steps. "But it doesn't make any difference."

Sierra stood frozen with surprise as she watched him go. Then she heard the roar of the motor and saw the Jeep backing recklessly out of the driveway. She was abruptly jarred out of her haze. She ran to the edge of the porch. "The hell it doesn't," she shouted after him. "Listen to me, York. It makes all the difference in the world." The Jeep was already halfway down the block and, if he heard her, he didn't respond. In another moment he was out of sight.

She was breathing hard and felt gloriously, wonderfully alive. After two weeks of hopelessness, at last she had something she could grasp and hold. As long as York loved her, she had a fighting chance, and until this minute she hadn't been sure he did care for her. She was too accustomed to dreams that hadn't come true to believe this most important one of her life had a chance of becoming a reality. Now she knew he *did* love her. They had a chance, and she'd be damned if she'd let it slip away. Canopy beds were one thing; York Delaney was something else entirely.

Why was he so certain they couldn't have a life together? she wondered. He was unshakably rigid in the belief that someday he'd wander off and leave her; he would let nothing pierce the fabric of that belief. There had to be some way she could convince him, but to do it she had to understand his thinking.

She slowly turned and sat down on the wooden swing. She leaned back, her gaze on the colorful town of Hell's Bluff, a town isolated from time. York's town. She heard again that faint ringing of memory. There was something there, if she could only reach out and touch it. This time, instead of dismissing the vague memory, she concentrated on trying to understand it.

Hell's Bluff. My kind of town, York had said. A boom town. Here today. Gone tomorrow. Like me.

That was it! She jerked up straight. It was so clear. Why hadn't she been able to put the pieces of the puzzle together before? She had been handed enough clues by Deuce and Kathleen, and even by York himself.

She jumped up from the swing and ran into the house. "Deuce!" she called as she tore up the stairs.

Deuce came out of the kitchen into the hall. He looked up at her, then glanced down at the full cup of coffee he was carrying. "Talk about narrow escapes," he said. He set the cup and saucer down on the oval table in the foyer. "What can I do for you?"

She stopped on the landing. "Can you arrange for another helicopter right away? I have to go somewhere."

His expression became wary. "We made a deal, Sierra."

"I'm not running away. In fact, I want you to come with me. Can you arrange for the helicopter?"

He nodded slowly. "It will take an hour or two to have one flown out from Tucson. Is that soon enough?"

She nodded. "That will be fine. Thanks, Deuce."

"May I ask where we're going?"

She glanced up at the portrait of Rising Star on the wall beside her. Was there the faintest hint of a smile on the Apache woman's lips? "Where it all started," she said softly. "Killara."

Ten

Deuce watched York cleaving through the water, his arms churning like the explosive arms of a steam engine. The white foam he was leaving in his wake was also reminiscent of steam, Deuce thought as he picked his way carefully across the wet tiles to the spot he estimated York's head would surface. He knew what York's reaction was going to be when he saw him and unconsciously braced himself. He wasn't disappointed.

"What the hell are you doing here?" York asked, frowning. He levered himself out of the pool and sat on its edge in one smooth movement. "I told you to stay with Sierra."

"So you did." Deuce tossed him a towel and squatted down beside him. "However, Sierra had a different idea. She sent me to you. Some time ago actually. I've been wandering around this bloody office building you call Delaney Tower for over an hour trying to find you. I went to the executive offices first and heard all about the crisis the three of you went through today. Then I tried the penthouse, but you weren't there. I went to the restaurant, and then I thought to try the gym." His lips thinned with annoyance. "You could have told someone where you'd gone. I'm not a bloodhound, you know. I don't—"

"Knock it off, Deuce," York said wearily as he began to dry his hair. "Believe me, I've had enough stress today without you picking at me."

"What really happened here? Police and—"

York held up his hand to stop him. "I'll tell you about it later. It was bad enough to go through that hell without having to describe it to all and sundry. You've found me. Now what's the message from Sierra?"

"Well, it's not exactly a message. It's more on the order of a summons."

York's hand froze in midmotion and his eyes darkened in concern. "What the hell do you mean, a summons? What's wrong with her? Is she sick again?"

"Easy. Don't go off in a tizzy. I didn't say she was sick." Deuce's gaze slid away from York to rest pensively on the high board at the far end of the pool. "Of course, I didn't say she wasn't, did I?"

"Dammit, Deuce. Stop playing games," York said between clenched teeth. "If you don't tell me why she wants me to come back to Hell's Bluff, I'm going to toss you into this pool."

"But she's not at Hell's Bluff. She left not long after you did."

Shock seemed to wrench his body as pain flooded through his entire being. He supposed he should have expected her to bolt after that last scene before he had left her. He had been in such an emotional maelstrom, he hadn't been able to think clearly. Thank heavens she hadn't disappeared entirely as he'd immediately feared. Deuce knew where she was. He was barely able to get the word past the tightness in his throat. "Where?"

"Did I tell you she received a letter from Chester Brady this morning?" Deuce asked. He was still not looking at York. "No? I don't see how that could have slipped my mind."

"Brady!" York threw the towel aside as he jumped to his feet. "Dammit, you let her go to Brady? Do you want to see her kill herself?"

"What you don't seem to understand is that people have the right to choose their own destinies, York. You can't save Sierra if she doesn't want to be saved." He paused. "And in Sierra's case you have no option but to let her go her own way. You've made it very clear you have no desire to be bound to her. You certainly can't have it both ways."

"Where is she?"

"Sierra's very independent and won't tolerate that type of ambiguity. I should think you'd realize tha— York! Dammit, put me down!"

York stepped closer to the pool, holding Deuce's slight body over the water. "Where?"

"Oh, very well. If you must use brute force, I have no recourse but to dispense with the rest of my lecture. Pity. I was just getting into the swing of it. Put me down."

As York set him back on his feet, Deuce meticulously tucked his tapered cowboy shirt back in his jeans. "I didn't say she was with Brady's troupe, merely that the opportunity was there."

"Deuce," York said, enunciating each word with menacing clarity, "I believe I'm going to murder you."

Deuce backed away hurriedly. "She's waiting for you at Killara. Not the homestead itself. She asked me to let her out on the high knoll in the foothills that overlooks most of the property."

"Killara! Why the hell would she go to Killara?"

Deuce shrugged. "She didn't confide in me. She just told me to tell you to come to her there. Are you going?"

"Of course, I'm going. You let her out alone in the foothills. Anything could happen to her. Since we've met her, she's come down with near pneumonia, been strangled by a python, almost raped in a brothel, and jumped from a trapeze." He turned and started toward the dressing rooms. "I don't dare guess what else is lurking on the horizon."

"Hmm." Deuce's faint smile held a trace of sly satisfaction. "Now that I think about it, when the pilot set the helicopter down, I did see something with gray fur streak by a cluster of rocks on the knoll. Are there wolves in the foothills of the Dragoons, by any chance?"

York muttered a low vengeful curse, but his stride unconsciously quickened.

Deuce's smile widened as he threw back his shoulders and sauntered after York. He could have been a bit more merciful perhaps, but York had needed a lesson. There were many ways a man of his size could deal with the brute force of the Goliaths of this world, and he had learned them all.

It was sunset by the time York arrived at Killara.

Sierra was sitting on top of the grassy knoll, her arms linked loosely around her drawn up legs. She was gazing at the distant homestead and the purple-shadowed grandeur of the Dragoon mountains beyond it. When the helicopter began to descend, she looked up and waved cheerfully. York darted an annoyed glance at Deuce as the pilot set the helicopter down.

"Not a wolf in sight," York said. "Amazing, isn't it?"

Deuce met his gaze with innocence. "It was a very predictable mistake. What could you expect from a one-eyed tenderfoot like me?"

"Chicanery, deceit, a touch of malice," York enumerated. "Shall I go on?"

"Please don't. You're making me blush." Deuce smiled. "She's waiting for you. If I didn't know better, I'd think that York, the dragon fighter, was a trifle nervous."

York opened the door of the helicopter and jumped to the ground. "Wait for us. I'm taking her back to Hell's Bluff."

Sierra drew a deep breath as she watched York walk toward her. She slowly got to her feet and wiped her palms on her jeans. It did little good. Her hands still felt cold and clammy with nervousness. He had changed from the business suit into his usual faded jeans and a navy-blue shirt. He no longer looked the stranger he had this morning, and that helped.

He stopped before her and thrust out his hand. "Come on, we're going back to Hell's Bluff. What the hell ever possessed you to have Deuce drop you here in the middle of nowhere? If you wanted to see Killara, you should have told me. We'll arrange to drop in at the homestead for dinner next week."

She shook her head. "No. Now, York. No polite social visit. It's time you came home."

"I don't know what you're talking about." He frowned fiercely. "And I don't think you do eith—" The roar of the helicopter drowned his words. He turned to see Deuce waving to him as the pilot lifted the aircraft off the ground. "What the devil! I told them to wait for us."

"And I told Deuce to leave us alone after he dropped you off. I must have been more insistent than you in expressing my wishes. He knew I needed time alone with you."

She ran her tongue across her suddenly dry lips. "I believe you were saying I didn't know what I was talking about. Well, you're wrong. I do know, but I didn't realize what the problem was for a long time. It took a while for it all to come together. I almost gave up and accepted your vision of the situation." She smiled shakily. "I guess that was natural. My self-image wasn't the greatest, and it was easy for me to believe I wouldn't be woman enough to hold you."

"Lord, Sierra, I never meant that." He took an impulsive step forward. "I don't know how you could even imagine I'd stop loving you. You're everything I would ever want in a woman; companion, mistress, beloved."

Joy, radiance, relief. The emotions flowing through her were so strong, she found it difficult to speak. "That's very good to know. It's going to make the rest of this a great deal easier."

Her dark eyes were gazing at him with such glowing intensity, he experienced a sense of déjà vu. That first night in his study she had looked at him like this and he had wanted to lay the world at her feet. He wanted to do the same thing now. "What do you want from me, Sierra?" he asked gently. "Why are you here?"

"I don't want anything from you. You've given me what I want. You love me." She smiled with a brilliance that made him catch his breath. "I want to give you something."

"What?"

"Your place." She gestured to the valley below. "Killara."

"I thought you said I carried my place around within me."

"You do, but that was Killara too. I didn't understand that." Her voice was earnest. "I don't think you do either. That's why you won't let yourself take what you want. That's why you won't give us a chance. You won't accept the fact you have a right to a place in life."

His body tautened with a strange tension. "I don't know what you mean."

"Yes, you do. Think about it. It all fits together. Remember what you told me your reaction was when you found out you were going to live after all? You said you went a little wild and were thrown off balance because it was difficult to believe in miracles. And after Kathleen told me about the heirloom clock you broke—"

"She said I broke the clock?" York interrupted. "I didn't break that blasted clock."

"You didn't?" she asked, surprised. "Kathleen didn't exactly say you broke it. I guess I just assumed . . ." She shrugged. "Well, it doesn't matter right now. She did say you fought the idea that you could never be a real part of the family or Killara, and that it took you a long time to accept it." She paused. "But you finally did accept it, didn't you? You had to, because otherwise you couldn't stand the pain. Then a miracle happened, and you found out everything you'd accepted was a lie. You could become brother, son, partner in Killara, everything you'd ever wanted." She smiled sadly. "But it was too late. Deuce said second thoughts are nearly impossible to accept, and he's right. You still had a lingering conviction you had no right to Killara, no right to life. So you left Killara and your family and lived a life you could accept. Even when your love for your family and Killara drew you home, you still held back. You built yourself a boom town on a mountaintop, a town with no roots and a question mark for a future. Here today, gone tomorrow." She let out a shaky breath. "Don't you see? You'll always live that life if you don't realize you have a right to everything Rafe and Burke possess. Oh, I don't mean the wealth and property, just the *belonging*. A place, York."

His eyes were glittering as he looked down at her. "You've thought a great deal about this, haven't you?" The words were husky and a little halting. "What if you're wrong? What if it's just the nature of the beast?"

"I'm not wrong," she said confidently. "But if I am, it still won't matter. You'll never get away from me now. I'll follow you to Hell's Bluff or the wilds of the Congo." She paused. "Or to Killara. You name it. Because, you see, I've found my place too. I'll never have a Killara, but I'll have what I am inside me." She took a step forward and slid her arms around his waist. She nestled close to him, rubbing her cheek contentedly against his chest. "And I'll have you, York. Love is a place too."

He stood absolutely motionless for an instant. Then his arms went around her and he was crushing her to him. His cheek pressed against her temple and it was damp with tears. "Yes, love is a place too." His big hands were unsteady as they caressed her hair. "I don't need Killara, Sierra. Not as long as I have you. I couldn't have let you go. Not ever. I kept telling myself I had to do it, but I don't think—" His voice broke. "Lord, I love you."

"Well, you certainly made us both miserable enough while you were fighting it," she grumbled. "We're just lucky I came to my senses in time. You know, I had to fight a few battles myself to get this far. Peacocks can be very intimidating to little brown hens."

"But you're not a brown hen." He pushed her away from him to look down at her. His face was lit with joy, exuberance, and a wild mischief. "You're a soaring flamingo." His hands encircled her waist and he lifted her high over his head as he spun in a dizzying circle. "You're a cardinal in the snow, you're a—"

She lovingly pressed her fingers to his lips and laughed down at him. "Peacock?"

He let her slide slowly down his body until his lips met hers sweetly, warmly, and with all the love in the world. He lifted his head. "Peacock."

"Okay, I'll accept that. We're both peacocks, spreading our plumage to an admiring populace." She kissed him again. "As one peacock to another, will you tell me something?"

"What?"

"Who broke the clock?"

He laughed, his eyes twinkling. "Now that's a Delaney family secret. It will require more than a birds-of-a-feather relationship to wrest the details of that episode from me."

"It will?"

He nodded. "Rafe, Burke, and I swore a solemn pact on Old Shamus's grave. They wouldn't understand if I let an outsider into the story." He lifted her chin, cradling her face in his hands and looking into her eyes. "There's only one thing to do. You'll have to marry me." He kissed her tenderly. "I'll tell you all the shocking details on our wedding day. Okay?"

"Okay," she whispered. She couldn't stand it. She was so happy, she felt as if she were going to float away into the stratosphere at any moment. "I wouldn't want you to break your promise. Shamus might suddenly decide to haunt the hallowed halls of Killara."

"It's a good thing you have a proper respect for our family honor as you're about to be absorbed into the Delaney menage yourself. Killara has a way of taking in strangers and making them belong to her."

"Like Rising Star?"

He nodded slowly. "Like Rising Star. We're going to have to bring her home. I don't think she'll be happy for much longer at Hell's Bluff."

Sierra tensed, then tried to relax. It was his decision. She couldn't make it for him. "No?"

For a moment he seemed troubled. "I don't know if you're right about me. You may be, but it's too early for me to tell yet. I do know that wherever I am, I want you to be there too. I do want Killara for you and my children." One finger traced the line of her cheekbone. "But I can live without Killara. I don't think I can live without you, Sierra."

She swallowed hard and firmly blinked back the tears. "You're not going to have to do without either one of us. I'm going to make sure—" She broke off and took a step back as she heard the sudden throb of a helicopter. She looked up to see one with the familiar Shamrock logo approaching Killara from the west. Her brow creased in puzzlement. "Deuce?"

York grinned. "No way. He wouldn't dare disobey a determined lady like Sierra Smith. No, it must be Rafe. Burke flew back to Killara hours ago."

Rafe was returning to Killara, York thought. As he watched his brother's helicopter heading for the homestead landing pad, he felt a strong sense of rightness. They were all returning to the source that had nurtured and given meaning and substance to the lives of generations of Delaneys. It must have been an instinct as ancient and mystical as nature itself to have influenced the three of them to gather at this time.

"York." Sierra's soft voice brought his attention back to her. Her eyes were glowing with understanding and love. "You're not odd man out any longer. Don't you think it's time we strolled down to join your brothers and you showed me this fabulous house I've heard so much about?"

He reached out slowly and took her hand. "Yes." He began to lead her down the twisting path to the valley. Killara was shining, strong and enduring in the scarlet glow of the setting sun, as it had through more than a century of sunsets. York felt his heart lift and a heady joy possess him. *Killara.* His clasp tightened on the small, vital hand of the woman who had given it back to him. *Sierra.* "Yes, love," he said. "It's time I took you home."

THE EDITOR'S CORNER

Home for the Holidays! Certainly home is the nicest place to be in this upcoming season . . . and coming home, finding a home, perfecting one are key elements in each of our LOVESWEPTs next month.

First, in Peggy Webb's delightful **SCAMP OF SALTILLO,** LOVESWEPT #170, the heroine is setting up a new home in a small Mississippi town. Kate Midland is a witty, lovely, committed woman whose determination to save a magnolia tree imperiled by a construction crew brings her into face-to-face confrontation with Saltillo's mayor, Ben Adams. What a confrontation! What a mayor! Ben is self-confident, sensual, funny, generous . . . and perfect for Kate. But it takes a wacky mayoral race—including goats, bicycles, and kisses behind the bandstand—to bring these two fabulous people together. A romance with real heart and humor!

It is their homes—adjacent apartments—that bring together the heroine and hero in **FINNEGAN'S HIDEAWAY,** LOVESWEPT #171, by talented Sara Orwig. Lucy Reardon isn't really accident prone, but try to convince Finn Mundy of that. From the moment he spots the delectable-looking Lucy, her long, long shapely legs in black net stockings, he is falling . . . for her, with her, even

(continued)

off a ladder on top of her! But what are a few bruises, a minor broken arm compared to the enchantment and understanding Lucy offers? When Finn's brothers—and even his mother—show up on the doorstep, the scene is set for some even wilder misunderstandings and mishaps as Finn valiantly tries to handle that mob, his growing love for Lucy, law school exams, and his failing men's clothing business. A real charmer of a love story!

In the vivid, richly emotional **INHERITED,** LOVE-SWEPT #172, by gifted Marianne Shock, home is the source of a great deal of the conflict between heroine Tricia Riley and hero Chase Colby. Tricia's father hires Texas cowboy Chase to run Tricia's Virginia cattle ranch. Their attraction is instantaneous, explosive . . . as powerful as their apprehensions about sharing the running of the ranch. He brings her the gift of physical affection, for she was a child who lost her mother early in life and had never known her father's embrace or sweet words. She gives Chase the gift of emotional freedom and, at last, he can confide feelings he's never shared. But before these two ardent, needy people can come together both must deal with their troublesome pasts. A love story you'll cherish!

In **EMERALD FIRE,** LOVESWEPT #173, that marvelous storyteller Nancy Holder gives us a delightful couple in Stacy Livingston and Keith

(continued)

Mactavish . . . a man and a woman who seem worlds apart but couldn't be more alike at heart. And how does "home" play a part here? For both Stacy and Keith home means roots—his are in the exotic land of Hawaii, where ancestors and ancient gods are part of everyday life. Stacy has never felt she had any real roots, and has tried to find them in her work toward a degree as a marine biologist. Keith opens his arms and his home to her, sharing his large and loving family, his perceptions of sensual beauty and the real romance of life. You'll relish this exciting and provocative romance!

Home for the Holidays . . . in every heartwarming LOVESWEPT romance next month. Enjoy. And have a wonderful Thanksgiving celebration in your home!

Warm wishes,

Carolyn Nichols

Carolyn Nichols
  Editor
LOVESWEPT
Bantam Books, Inc.
666 Fifth Avenue
New York, NY 10103

His love for her is madness.
Her love for him is sin.

Sunshine
and
Shadow

by Sharon and Tom Curtis

COULD THEIR EXPLOSIVE LOVE BRIDGE THE CHASM BETWEEN TWO IMPOSSIBLY DIFFERENT WORLDS?

He thought there were no surprises left in the world ... but the sudden appearance of young Amish widow Susan Peachey was astonishing—and just the shock cynical Alan Wilde needed. She was a woman from another time, innocent, yet wise in ways he scarcely understood.

Irresistibly, Susan and Alan were drawn together to explore their wildly exotic differences. And soon they would discover something far greater—a rich emotional bond that transcended both of their worlds and linked them heart-to-heart ... until their need for each other became so overwhelming that there was no turning back. But would Susan have to sacrifice all she cherished for the uncertain joy of their forbidden love?

"Look for full details on how to win an authentic Amish quilt displaying the traditional 'Sunshine and Shadow' pattern in copies of SUNSHINE AND SHADOW or on displays at participating stores. No purchase necessary. Void where prohibited by law. Sweepstakes ends December 15, 1986."

Look for SUNSHINE AND SHADOW in your bookstore or use this coupon for ordering: